WINSOME

FOURSOME

WINSOME

FOURSOME

ASHLEY LAINO

www.blkdogpublishing.com

Dedicated to my amigops, Merideth Hinton and Alicia Altemose. Thanks for being there through all my ups, downs, and awkward teenage crushes.

Also by Ashley Laino for your consideration:

A Storm of Magic

Being brought back from the dead is an impressive trick, even for magician Darien Burron. Now he must try and use his sleight of hand to swindle modern-day witch, Mirah, to sign her power away, or end up a tormented demon in the afterlife.

Meanwhile, sixteen-year-old Mirah is starting to lose control of her powers. After an incident at her aunt's Witchery store, Mirah is sent to a secret coven to learn to control her abilities. While away, Mirah meets up with a soft-spoken clairvoyant, a brazen storm witch, and the creator of dark magic itself. The young woman must learn to trust in herself before she loses herself entirely to the darkness that hunts her.

there is something
almost unearthly
about the friendship
between girls,
isn't there?

all they ever want to do is
protect, protect, protect.
fiercely now.
fiercely now.
my advice for you:
don't take her for granted.
ever.

-Amanda
Lovelace

CHAPTER ONE:
JACKIE
A DUSTY DISCOVERY

"Archie, can you please stop chewing on Mr. Feet?!"

Jackie sighed as she leaned against the dusty wall of her attic. It was mid-August, and the room was so hot Jackie could feel beads of sweat rolling down her back, even though she had only been there for a few seconds.

It had been years since Jackie had last stepped foot into her attic, but with a new baby sister on the way, her mom had sent her upstairs to try and retrieve a box of old baby clothes. Jackie had the feeling that her mother was just looking for an excuse to get her out of the way so that she could gossip on the phone with Jackie's Aunt Patsy in peace.

But Jackie didn't mind. With the summer ending, she was starting to run out of things to do. She had already explored every inch of her yard for lost treasure or secrets and kicked around every ball in her house. Video games never interested her, and even though she had an unread pile of books calling her name, she found it was too hot to sit and focus for long.

Normally in desperate times of boredom like these, she'd call on one of her best friends to come over and save her, but Sam had summer classes, Kylie was babysitting, and Teresa was at some soccer jock camp every day this week.

So, when her mom offered her the chance for an adventure (well, more of a chore, but Jackie convinced herself anything could be an adventure if one had the right mindset), she jumped at the chance.

So, followed as always by her faithful bulldog Archie, Jackie journeyed into the heat wave that was her attic.

She knew she was too old to play with stuffed animals, but that didn't mean she was comfortable letting Archie tear Mr. Feet apart. Even though his stomach almost dragged on the wooden floor, Archie saw Jackie's advances as an opportunity for a rousing game of tag and began sprinting around the room as fast as his stubby little legs could carry him.

"Drop it!" Jackie cried as she lunged forward but, not known for her natural grace, she stumbled over her own feet and careened into a pile of cardboard boxes stacked precariously in the corner of the room.

After the dust had subsided, she let out a groan of frustration as Archie continued to prance around the attic, clearly proud of his antics.

"Great, now I'm going to have to clean all of this," she complained. Archie stared back unsympathetically with a tilted head, the rabbit still dangling from his mouth.

Deciding to give up on the war for Mr. Feet, Jackie bent down and started reorganizing the odds and ends that had tumbled out of their boxes. There were old photos of when she was a baby, along with some papers from when her mom was in college. But at least she discovered which box held her old baby clothes, so she shoved a few onesies that had fallen onto the floor back into the box and moved it aside for later.

Finally, panting and drenched in sweat, Jackie finished cleaning up the mess of cardboard. When she turned around, she saw that Archie had fully ripped a foot off Mr. Feet and was going to town tearing the stuffing out of it.

Jackie abandoned any hope of saving the beloved stuffed animal, grabbed the box of clothes, and was about to go back downstairs in defeat. As she made her way across the floor, she accidentally kicked a tennis ball she must have missed, and she watched with exhausted amusement as Archie abandoned his stuffed prize and scurried over to chase it as it bounced against the attic wall. Jackie turned away, calling for Archie to follow her.

Instead of Archie's tiny nails pitter-pattering after her, Jackie heard him let out a low whine as he scratched against something along the wall.

"What's up, buddy?" she asked, placing the box on the ground.

In response, Archie barked and began clawing more frantically at a space along the edge of the attic floor.

Crouching on the ground, Jackie noticed a small space between the floor and the wall. Intrigued, she ran her hand along the old wood until she noticed the faint outline of a cubby space that had been sealed and hidden away years ago. For reasons she didn't understand, she felt her heart start to pound faster, and her hands started to tremble as she pushed against the small door.

It didn't budge. Nope, not even a little bit. She pushed harder and harder, and even though particles of dirt started to fly away and the outline of the door became clearer, there was still no sign of anything starting to open.

She rubbed her hand again and again over the space in search of some sort of handle or keyhole, but there was nothing to be found.

With a huff, she leaned back, then threw her shoulder against the door as hard as she could. The door flew open, and with a squeak, Jackie fell forward. Before she could regain her composure, Archie, who had hurried over to see what all the noise was about, had half his body engulfed in the pitch darkness of the cubby hole.

"Archie!" Jackie squealed with fright, and she wrenched him out of the darkness.

For his part, Archie seemed unharmed, but between his teeth he held what appeared to be an old leather notebook.

Intrigued, Jackie slowly reached her hand into the small, dark space and carefully felt around for any other treasures that might be found. There was no such luck. There was nothing else in the crawlspace. Slightly disappointed, she removed the notebook from Archie's clutches and began flipping through the pages.

Even though someone had tucked it away for heaven knows how long, the cover was strangely free from dirt. The brown leather gleamed as if she had just picked the book up new at the local bookstore. There was no title or words of any kind. The only decoration was a faint gold binding string along the book's spine.

Flipping through one more time, Jackie found that the pages, though slightly yellowed from age, were still in good shape and clear of dirt or water marks.

She didn't know what she hoped to find in this notebook, but she figured that it must have some sort of importance if it was hidden away so carefully. But sadly, every single page was blank.

Sweaty and exhausted, Jackie determined her adventure into the attic was a bust. As she grabbed the box of baby clothes, she tossed the old notebook on top of the pile. School was about to start again, and she figured that at least this notebook would make taking notes more interesting. She could pretend she was a witch jotting down her spells for generations to come, which seemed a lot more exciting than just writing down the week's spelling words in a boring spiral ring notebook.

"Archie, come!" Jackie cried over her shoulder, and without hesitation Archie clumsily bounded down the steps. Jackie followed him, wondering how long it would be before dinner, as all this attic mayhem had given her quite an appetite.

Deep in daydreams about spaghetti and fresh loaves of garlic bread, she didn't notice the chubby door slowly close itself behind her. And as she flicked the light off, she didn't see that behind her was a light trail of gold dust following her as she stumbled down to her living room.

CHAPTER TWO:
TERESA
A DAY OF SPRAINED ANKLES
AND BRUISED EGOS

Teresa was in agony. There was no way she would ever be able to recover.

Ok, if she was being realistic, Teresa was on some good pain medication, so she wasn't actually in that much physical pain. But the emotional pain, why, that was almost too much to handle.

Teresa had sprained her ankle, which meant that she wouldn't be able to play soccer or really any sport for almost six weeks!

She had decided that she was going to lose her mind. There was no way around it. Having to sit on her butt and watch her teammates get better while she weakened day after day was a fate worse than death. Sports weren't just a hobby to Teresa. Sports were her life. They were what got her up in the morning and gave her purpose.

Teresa hated school. The words in the textbooks seemed to fly right out of her head as soon as she read them, so she could never remember anything that was going on, and the numbers in math seemed like a different language.

Starting in first grade, Teresa's teachers noted that

she was a 'struggling' learner. They sent her to the guidance office and to tiny classrooms where she had to take test after test in order to assess her 'needs.'

On suggestion from the school, Teresa's parents took her to specialists who made her read the same boring passages over and over again. Then they shipped her over to one doctor who gave her pills that made her sleepy and then to another doctor who gave her pills that made her so hyper that she would stay up until two in the morning, cleaning her room because she couldn't get herself to close her eyes, let alone actually fall asleep. Some claimed that she had ADD, and another so-called expert said it was something called Auditory Processing Disorder, but Teresa knew the secret truth was that she was just plain dumb.

For ages she would try to hide this fact by refusing to read when teachers called on her or making up lies as to why she never had her homework done. Her grades dropped, and she was called into parent-teacher conferences where her parents would despair over not knowing what to do with her. Teachers labeled her a 'difficult' student, and it seemed that Teresa's life had nowhere to go but down.

Most of her special classes didn't even give her comfort. In art, the best she could muster was a particularly expressive set of stick figures, and since she was completely tone-deaf, music was certainly not going to be a strong suit. Then there was one shining beacon of hope. Gym. Gym was the only class in Teresa's day where she didn't feel like a complete failure. In fact, she found at a fairly early age that this was the one area where she excelled beyond her classmates. Basketball, softball, soccer, tennis, no matter the sport, Teresa took to it like a fish in water.

Teachers used her as an example for the other students. Coaches would look at her with gleaming eyes as they thought about the state championships she could bring them. The girls stopped making fun of her as much, and the boys hung around her, trying to subtly pick up tips on how they could improve their free throws and football spirals.

Teresa found her niche, and things started to look up for her. Even her grades started to improve because she had to keep them up in order to participate in the games. She should finally start being happy, shouldn't she?

There was only one problem. Teresa never got to have classes with any of her friends.

Jackie read like a book a day, and Sam was practically a certified genius, so they were always in the brainiac classes. Even Kylie, who was closer to Teresa's speed, was in the average classes, while Teresa was always shoved in with the 'remediation' students, but everyone knew that 'remediation' was just code for the 'dumb kid class'.

The classroom was tucked away from the rest of the students. and there were two teachers instead of one because they were the kids who needed "extra assistance."

Every year, Teresa would look around at the loud-mouthed boys and the dead-eyed girls she had to sit next to for years before and wonder how she ended up in this situation. But at least she always had some sport after school to look forward to.

Now as she lay on her couch, with her foot propped up on a pillow, and the first day of seventh grade lurking around the corner, Teresa felt particularly depressed, and not even her favorite reality TV show, *Rich Boat Drama*, could cheer her up.

"Hooonnnnnneeeey!" Teresa's mom called from the next room, "I have a surprise for you!"

"Great," Teresa responded unenthusiastically, not moving her eyes from the screen until she felt spastic bouncing coming from the other side of the sofa.

Wincing, Teresa turned to see Jackie clutching some brown book in her arms and grinning at her like a maniac. "I came over as soon as I heard that you were home. I'm sorry about your ankle, but are you ready for the best year of your life?" Jackie practically squealed. Her dark bob bounced as she hopped up and down.

"Is your plan to have me pass out from the pain? I

guess if I'm unconscious then I may have some fun."

Jackie squeaked out an apology, and Teresa couldn't help but smile. Jackie, Kylie, and Teresa had played on the same traveling soccer team when they were little. Each of them was a little odd in their own way. Since the other girls didn't really want to talk to them, they soon befriended each other, first out of need, but soon became inseparable. A year later, Jackie brought Sam into their mix, and the 'winsome foursome' was born.

"Seriously though," Jackie continued, leaning forward, her eyes gleaming, "Are you ready for your mind to be absolutely blown?"

"Listen, Jackie. You've tried to get me to read your books before. I'm sure it's great, but I'll just wait for the movie to come out."

"It's not a book you read!" Jackie hissed as she inched herself off the couch. Teresa waited expectantly as Jackie peered over each shoulder. Once she was sure they would not be overheard, she whispered giddily to Teresa, "It's a wish granter!"

Teresa rolled her eyes and sank further into the couch cushions, "Don't you think we're getting a bit old to be playing pretend? I'm not exactly in any shape for your adventures, Jackie."

Jackie shook her head and shoved the notebook closer to Teresa, "It's not pretend, I swear. I found this book hidden away in my attic, and I thought it was lame at first, too. But then I started writing in it, you know, kind of just using it as a journal, and, I swear to God, whatever wish you write down in this notebook ends up coming true one way or another!"

With a snort of disbelief, Teresa picked up the notebook and flipped through it. When she finished, she tossed the book back at Jackie. "Oh, it's magic, alright, magically blank. I'm sorry for being mean, but I'm really not in the mood for a speech about how we can write about our wishes and make them come true with our imaginations on paper. It's real or bust for me right now."

Teresa felt bad for raining on Jackie's parade, but to her surprise, she saw that Jackie's smile didn't waver. In fact, her eyes seemed to gleam even more mischievously than before.

"Oh, this isn't imagination," Jackie grinned, "And I can prove it. I'd even be willing to bet on it."

Biting her lip, Teresa picked up the notebook once again. Teresa loved bets, and this seemed like an easy one to win. "Fine. Prove it." Teresa ordered.

Jackie, practically vibrating with excitement, flipped open the notebook and pulled out a pen from her pocket. "So," she asked gleefully, as she passed the pen to Teresa, "What is it you wish for?"

CHAPTER THREE:
SAM
THE TIME SAM DIDN'T CARE
ABOUT THE ANSWERS

"What I'm telling you is that I put my daughter in your school so that she can be challenged. She has always had the best math PSSA scores in her grade, and now because of one little blip, you're trying to tell me that math is too hard for her?! She's just being challenged for the first time. How do you expect these kids to succeed in college or the workforce if you don't push them?"

Groaning, Sam raised the volume of her music, desperately trying to drown out the sound of her mother tearing into her school's guidance office for not putting her in the highest math class this year.

Sam was 'gifted', or at least that's what she had been told since she was in third grade, and boy, was her mother thrilled to hear this piece of news. She loved her mom, she really did, and she knew that in her own way, her mother meant well, but she had always been... a bit much.

When Sam was in first grade, her mom was already making plans for college. By second grade, her entire life was planned out for her. She was going to go to an Ivy League college and become a mechanical engineer since her math scores were always at the top of the class. Then at thirty, she would get married to a man who made the same amount as her, if not more, with two children following promptly after the wedding.

Finally, they would all go to Disney World and live happily ever after, and her mom would always have the most bragging rights at the church bake sales. This was the dream, and Sam's mother would do anything to make it a reality.

She worked hard to make sure Sam had the best resume possible. Although she initially wanted Sam to excel in two sports, she quickly realized that sports were not Sam's strongest suit, so she promptly changed her plan accordingly. Instead, on Wednesdays there were Mandarin classes. Thursdays it was cello lessons, 'Little Achiever' camps over the summer, and frequent church community projects All to make Sam appear 'well rounded'.

Everything was in place for Sam to succeed. There was only one little issue; Sam's mother never stopped to consider how Sam felt about all of this. Since turning twelve, Sam found that she didn't want any of it. School had always come easily to her, that much was true. But even though her math grades were excellent, the class always bored her to tears. Mandarin made her eyes glaze over, and if she could, she would cut every string of her cello and throw it right out the window. There were really only three things that made her truly happy; her friends, her music, and art.

Sam loved art. She loved every bit of it. She adored the acrylic and oily smell of the art room. She loved the feeling of a paintbrush in her hand and how she could lose herself for hours bent over a piece of canvas or drawing paper. She knew in her heart that she didn't want to be an engineer. She wanted to be an artist. It didn't matter to her whether she was an art teacher, a gallery owner, or just a caricature artist on the street. She just wanted art to be a part of her life.

When Sam heard the previous year that they were offering art classes at a local pottery studio, she begged her mother to switch one of her cello lessons for the class. She even tried to connect art and engineering and how the class would be perfect for her future, but her mother wouldn't hear a word of it.

Her mother accepted her drawings as a sweet side hobby, but she looked down on the arts as a frivolous path. So of course, she gave Sam a firm, respectful no, which led to a heartbroken Sam making a drastic decision. If she couldn't have her dreams, then neither could her mother. When it came time for the yearly state test, Sam deliberately bombed it. She bombed it hard. When the school and her mother got the scores, they were utterly bewildered. How could a student who had gotten As in Honors math all year and was on a high school math level fail so miserably on the test?

Sam's mother was even more shocked to learn Honors classes were determined by standardized testing. This meant for the first time in Sam's middle school career, she wasn't going to be in the highest class. She was going to be with the 'average' kids. The school might as well have told her mom that her daughter had been expelled; she was horrified.

The principal was called, her math teacher was called, and the guidance was currently being screamed at. At one point, she even threatened to call the state office and try to have Sam retake the test. Sam smiled, just a bit. She hated upsetting her mom; she really did. But she couldn't help taking some small pleasure in her rebellion.

A beep on her phone interrupted Sam's thoughts. She figured a text message from Jackie could wait, and she slid the notification away without even bothering to read the message. She leaned against her pillow and closed her eyes, ready to sink into her cocoon of music, when another beep interrupted her jam. One beep was followed by another and then another, until Sam couldn't ignore her friend any longer. To her surprise, Sam saw it wasn't just Jackie who was bombarding her with texts, Teresa seemed desperate to talk to her too.

> *Jackie-*
> *Sammmmmmmmmmmmmmmmmmmmmmmmmmmmm!*
> *We need*
> *to c u. ASAP!!!!!!!!! Super important news!*

> *Jackie-*
> *Seriously! Ur life is going to change! Call*
> *meeeeeeeeeee!!!!!!!!*

> *Teresa*
> *Sam we gotta talk big nws. can we c u?*

Biting the nail on her thumb, Sam continued to scroll through her messages. It didn't take a lot to get Jackie worked up about things, but Teresa usually only got this pumped when she scored a goal. She called Jackie, and the phone only rang once before Jackie picked it up.

"Ohmygodwhereareyouweneedtoseeyoucanwecom eover!"

Sam pulled the phone away from her ear so she wouldn't become completely deaf, listening to Jackie's babbling screeches. Once it seemed that Jackie had taken a breath, Sam returned the phone to her ear.

"What's going on? Is Teresa with you?"

"Yes! She's sitting next to me as we speak! We need to see you! This is something that I can't tell you over the phone. You need to see this in person! Can we stop by?!" Sam bit harder on her nail and removed her headphones. Her mom was still ranting, but she seemed to have moved on from verbally assaulting Sam's guidance counselor to lamenting the stupidity of everyone around her to Sam's father. There was no chance that her mom was going to let her have her friends over right now, but if she played her cards right with her dad, there was a chance she might be able to escape the house.

Fingers crossed, Sam furiously messaged Jackie:

Sam-
  My house is no good right now. But can we meet at the park a block down in like 20?

Jackie's response flashed across Sam's screen in a matter of seconds"

Jackie-
  Well make it work. We're trying to grab kylie too!!! Cya soon! Be PUMMMMMMPPPPPPPPEED!!!

Sam grinned and shoved her earbuds and phone into her pocket. Then, carefully, she inched her way down the hall, listening for her moment to strike.

A few seconds later, Sam heard her mom let out a final groan of disgust, followed by the tell-tale sound of her footsteps making their way to the bedroom so she could lie down with one of her 'stress headaches'. Once the door clicked shut and the whirl of the fan kicked on, Sam scurried over to her dad, who, as expected, was sitting at the kitchen table calmly drinking a cup of tea.

"What's up, Sammy spammy?" Sam's dad asked, invoking a pet name he had used for her since she was five and that she started hating when she turned ten. But desperate times called for desperate measures, so, swallowing her pride, Sam ignored the ridiculous nickname and instead gave her dad one of her most winning smiles.

"Hey, dad! The girls want to meet at the park in a little bit to go over our class schedule for this year. It's kind of like an end-of-summer meet-up. Can I go, please? It's right down the road, and I promise I'll be home for dinner; my room is clean, my Mandarin homework is done, and I'd really, really, really appreciate it."

She stood there with her hands clasped together in

prayer while her dad barely looked up from his mug.

"Sure, Spammy. Sounds nice. Besides, I don't think your mother's in any mood to cook, so it's probably going to be a pizza night. Have fun! Just get home before dark. You know how your mother is!"

With a sigh of relief, she gave her dad a quick hug before she sprinted out of the door. At this point, Sam didn't care if Jackie wanted to show her a jar of spiders; anything had to be better than being at her house right now. Practically skipping, she hurried her way to the park with the warm summer sun beating down on her neck and the unknown waiting happily in front of her.

CHAPTER FOUR:
KYLIE
WHEN THE ORDINARY STARTS
TO FEEL EXTRAORDINARY

Jackie was dragging Kylie by the arm, out the door, and down the road.

Kylie had no idea where she was going, and was perfectly fine with this fact. Growing up, Jackie was always pulling Kylie and her other friends one way or another in search of some great adventure and Kylie was always down for the ride.

Teresa and Sam were sometimes annoyed with Jackie's boundless enthusiasm, but Kylie never cared. She just liked feeling like she was a part of something. It was nice not to feel completely invisible once in a while.

Being one of seven kids made it very difficult to stand out at home, especially since Kylie was smack dab in the middle, child number four.

Her parents meant well, they really did, and she knew that they loved all of their children, but sometimes it was hard for them to keep track. Kylie was used to being called her sibling's name or always wearing her sister's hand-me-downs. Those things Kylie could forgive.

What drove her crazy was when her parents picked

her up late because they completely forgot she had soccer practice, or how her parents always had her babysit her younger siblings because her older siblings were too busy being amazing and perfect in every way.

Her oldest brother, John, was a senior and the most popular guy in school. He was the quarterback of the football team, and everyone was convinced he would win homecoming king.

Meanwhile her sister Clara, a junior, was in line to be valedictorian of her class. Even worse, with her honey-blonde hair and big blue eyes, every boy she met fell in love with her instantly.

Following Clara was Robert, who lately had been going by Roberto, but Kylie refused to call him that. He was a freshman and musical prodigy.

Robert sang like an angel and could play any instrument handed to him. Every year, her parents would herd their team of children to one music hall or another. Kylie would have to force herself to stay awake as Robert thrilled beautiful song after song, all wrapped up with a round of applause and tossed flowers onto the stage.

Kylie was average. Awkwardly and painfully average. Even her younger siblings had something going for them. Her little brother was hilarious and a delightful troublemaker, even at seven. There was five-year-old Tina, who was already showing signs of being a great little actor in her Tots for Talent shows at the local playhouse.

True, Brad, the youngest of the family, hadn't shown any signs of greatness, but since he was only three, it was just a matter of time before he learned to excel at something.

She wasn't the dumbest kid in her grade, but she wasn't the smartest. She didn't think she was hideous, but she certainly wasn't the prettiest girl in their grade, especially after discovering she needed glasses in the third grade. She was fine at sports, but not a top athlete. she wasn't particularly musical or artistic, and she wasn't especially funny or clever. She was just plain old boring Kylie as far as her family was concerned.

But Kylie knew she had something that no one in her family had. She had three incredible friends, and Kylie would go to the ends of the world with them if that is what they needed.

When Jackie and Teresa showed up around dinner, knocking furiously on the door and grinning like maniacs, Kylie didn't hesitate to let them through the door.

When they pulled her by the arm and demanded they bike to Feltsville Park, Kylie called for Robert to put down his violin for once and babysit the siblings.

There was a grunt of response, which was enough for Kylie to beeline out the door. She didn't bother asking questions, even though Teresa had texted them a day ago she had sprained her ankle, but now was riding behind Kylie as if nothing had happened.

All Kylie cared about right now was pushing one pedal after the other as the wind whipped her dark brown hair back and the late summer sun shone down on it.

For a moment, Kylie closed her eyes and lifted her hands off the faded steering bars. Letting the sound of her friend's laughter fill her ears, for a brief second Kylie felt free as a bird. If she could have, she would have flown away to some tropical island or iced mountain top. She would soar around the Earth and back again.

Jackie's screech of excitement broke Kylie from her trance as they biked up to the park entrance.

Sitting on a nearby bench was Sam, sitting with her freckled arms crossed over her chest, her face pursed in pretend annoyance.

"You're late!" Sam called to them as they walked their bikes toward the bench.

"Sorry, we had to get Kylie," Teresa explained.

"And we wanted everyone together for this moment," Jackie added.

Sam raised her pale eyebrows, "Well, whatever you have to tell us, you better say it quick. If I'm not home before dark, my mother will actually file a missing person's report on me."

Everyone nodded and hurried over to the nearest picnic table. Sam's curfew was no joke, and more than once their parents got a hysterical call from Sam's mom asking about her whereabouts.

Kylie, on the other hand, was in no rush whatsoever, as she was pretty sure that she could disappear for at least seventy-two hours before her parents noticed her absence.

Once they were all seated, Jackie unzipped her purple sequined backpack and pulled a plain-looking leather notebook out, placing it carefully on the table as if it were made of glass.

As Jackie made sure she had all their attention, she spread her arms open in a grand gesture, "Teresa, you already understand the magic that sits before us, but Kylie and Sam, I hope you're ready for this."

Sam leaned closer to the notebook, "Does it like have the answers for this year's tests or something? Because that would technically be cheating and...."

"It's better than any old test answers," Teresa replied, gently swinging her foot back and forth.

"I thought you had sprained your ankle," Sam remarked, slightly startled.

"Exactly," Teresa answered, and she and Jackie exchanged a mysterious grin.

Jackie went on to tell Kylie and Sam the tale of how she came across this notebook.

"At first, I was going to use it as, like, a notebook for school, but then I figured that it was too cool to be used for, like, writing down science formulas. So, I was going to use it as a journal,"

Jackie then flipped open the notebook, and to Kylie's disappointment, she saw that the pages inside were blank.

"But when I went to write in it...." Jackie then pulled out a purple pen from her pocket, which wasn't unusual since

Jackie carried a pen in her pocket at all times, no matter what, "Look what happens."

In her loopy handwriting, Jackie wrote the words, "Hi! My name is Jackie." Seconds later, the words began to take on a golden glow and gleamed up from the page.

Sam's mouth dropped open, and Kylie lurched back in her seat as if she was afraid that the words would jump off the page and bite her.

"How is that possible?!" Sam gasped, "Is there some sort of electronic in the book, or maybe it has something to do with the ink from your pen? Maybe it's some sort of chemical reaction."

Sam babbled on, theorizing what could be causing the phenomenon. Kylie wanted to add something, she really did, but she just couldn't find the words.

"Oh, there's more," Jackie's dark eyes sparkled before she continued, "So, of course, I started freaking out. I didn't know if this was like, magic or if I was having a heat stroke. So, I kept writing, and the words kept glowing. Then I decided to push it a bit further, and I wrote down a wish, just to see what would happen."

"What did you wish for?" Kylie sputtered as she pushed her glasses up her nose.

"I didn't want to put down anything too serious at first, so I just wrote that I wished mom would take us out for ice cream after dinner."

"Did she?" Kylie asked.

"Yes! It was awesome!" Jackie wheezed.

Sam paused and rolled her eyes, "That could have just been a lucky coincidence."

"True," Jackie responded, "But then explain to me that when I wrote the words, they glowed so bright, I had to turn away, and then they disappeared into the book!!!"

"It's true," Teresa added, "Jackie came over to my house earlier, and I wrote that I wished for my ankle to be healed, and look at me!" she kicked her foot again,

"Prove it," Sam dared, and Jackie handed the pen

over to her.

"Don't go too crazy," Teresa warned, "My mom is still tweaking over my ankle."

"What did you tell her?" Kylie laughed.

"I told her that the doctors must have been wrong and that I just pinched it or something. I mean, I'm not a hundred percent yet, but at least I can move around," Teresa responded with an impish grin.

"When Teresa's mom saw her dancing around, her eyes practically bugged out of her head," Jackie added

"She thought I had faked the injury at first," Teresa added.

"But then she realized that Teresa would never try and get out of playing sports," Jackie giggled.

"So, she figured the doctors must have been wackos. She was so stunned that when I asked to leave with Jackie, she didn't even bother to fight me on it; she was too busy scratching her head."

Jackie and Teresa burst into a few peals of giggles while Sam and Kylie grinned at one another.

Kylie watched Sam twirl the pen in her hand. Kylie knew Sam almost better than Sam knew herself. Sam couldn't help but try and look at the logical parts of things. It was one of her greatest faults and would often cause her friends, especially Jackie, to sigh at her. Right now, Kylie knew that Sam was trying to find a scientific explanation for all of this and was drawing a blank.

"I..." Sam stammered. Kylie could practically see the gears in Sam's head turning, "I can't think of a wish right now. Kylie, you go."

Sam practically shoved the pen into Kylie's hand, and then she hopped over to the other side of the bench so that Kylie was now the one face-to-face with the magic notebook.

Kylie bit her lip. What would she wish for? There were too many things to choose from. She wished she were as smart as Sam or as athletic as Teresa. She wished she was as creative as Jackie or as pretty as her older sister.

She wished she was an only child and that her family were millionaires so she didn't have to wear her sister's hand-me-downs, that they could go out to eat every night, and never have to have her mom's nasty tuna fish casserole ever again. But most of all, what Kylie really wanted was to make an impression. To somehow stand out from her siblings in one way or another.

But all of those seemed too much, and Jackie and Teresa had told her not to go too far. So, Kylie wrote down the first thing that popped into her head.

"I wish that I didn't have to wear glasses anymore."

For a second, all four girls breathlessly stared down at the purple ink shining against the yellowed page. In a moment of breathtaking brilliance, the letters took on a golden sheen and lit up the page. Sure enough, each letter seemed to disappear into the book until it was like Kylie hadn't written anything at all.

All four girls sat silent and motionless, staring at the page. No one wanted to be the first one to break the spell. Teresa, who never could sit still for long, turned dramatically to Kylie wide-eyed.

"Well?"

Carefully, Kylie removed her glasses and placed them down on the table.

At first, the world was blurry, just as it always had been for her, but slowly, the world started to clear up before her.

"Kylie..." Sam whispered nervously.

"Guys," Kylie gasped, gently touching her eyelids and the corner of her eyes, "I can see."

CHAPTER FIVE:
JACKIE
THE WINSOME FOURSOME
MAKES AN OATH

The girls screamed so loud that an old woman walking her dog stopped in her tracks to glare at them.

"Are you serious?!" Sam wheezed, "You're not just lying to try to make us happy, right?

"How many fingers am I holding up?" Teresa asked.

"Three," Kylie giggled.

The girls unleashed another squeal of delight.

"This is amazing!" Jackie squeaked.

"We can do anything we want!" Teresa yelled, "I'll never have to study for another test in my life!"

"We can make all the boys in school fall in love with us," Kylie added, her eyes gleaming.

"I can finally get my mom off my back," Sam sighed.

Kylie, Sam, and Teresa continued to rattle off all of the amazing things that could be at their fingertips, thanks to the glorious new notebook.

"We could be millionaires!"

"We could be models!"

"I could be on varsity as a freshman!"

"We need a manifesto!"

"A what?" Kylie asked wide-eyed.

Jackie, who was usually grinning from ear to ear, looked uncharacteristically serious as she gently caressed the notebook, "A manifesto. Like, a list of rules. I mean, don't get me wrong. I'm beyond excited. But I was just thinking as you guys were talking that we don't really know anything about this notebook. We don't know what will happen if we just go wild with this. I mean, remember the diary from Harry Potter? What if this is the remnant of a soul from an evil wizard, and eventually, it'll possess us, and we'll unleash a giant snake onto the middle school?"

"Depends, can we control who the snake attacks?" Teresa wondered.

"Seriously!" Jackie cried, "What if there is a limit to how many wishes we can make, or what if every time we make a wish someone across the world dies or something? We should probably give ourselves some boundaries."

"Jackie does have a point," Sam added, "Also, we don't want other people knowing about this, or everyone's going to want to have a piece."

"We should write them in the notebook. You know, make it super official." Teresa suggested.

"This is very *Sisterhood of the Traveling Pants*," Jackie laughed, referencing one of her favorite book series.

"Yeah, but this is a lot more to the point than those pants." Sam pointed out.

"And didn't they have a rule where they weren't allowed to wash the pants? This is a lot more hygienic."

The debate began over how many rules they were going to have and why. There was still so much they didn't know about this newfound power, but Jackie couldn't help grinning at all of the endless possibilities that lay in front of them.

Finally, the sun started to set, and Sam started to panic about her curfew, so a final decision was made about the rules.

There were six rules in total. Teresa wanted five, but

Sam had a thing about even numbers. Jackie wanted ten, but Kylie said that they didn't want to overwhelm themselves, and this way there was room to grow.

It was determined that Sam had the best handwriting, so there in the notebook, written as clear as day in purple ink, were the rules:

The Official Rules of the Magic Notebook as Decreed by the Winsome Foursome:

1. To be fair, the notebook will rotate among the four of us on a weekly basis. The rotation will go: Jackie, Teresa, Sam, then Kylie. The new rotation starts every Friday.
2. Each girl will be allowed to make one wish in the notebook per week. If no wish is made, you can't save it up.
3. Wishes will follow genie rules: No wishing death on anyone and no wishing for more wishes.
4. You must write down what happened to you that week in the notebook. This is for scientific documentation.
5. It is FORBIDDEN to discuss the notebook with anyone outside of the winsome foursome. Make sure any wish you make you has a reasonable explanation for.
6. Treat the notebook with care and secrecy. Make sure to put it in a safe place that you will not forget (Jackie,) away from siblings that will tear out its pages (Kylie,) dirty soccer cleats (Teresa,) and most importantly, away from the eyes of prying mothers (Sam.)

Teresa said that they should make an oath with blood to solidify the rules, but Sam fainted at the sight of blood, so that was out. Kylie recommended that they spit shake on it, but that made Jackie want to barf. In the end, with an official handshake, elbow bump and finger snap, the rules of the notebook (a fancier name to be determined later) were decided on.

Jackie had already made her wish, but they decided that the easiest thing would be if Jackie held on to the notebook until next Friday.

All of this was fine with Jackie, who waved goodbye to her friends, feeling more excited and powerful now than at any time in her life.

Carefully, she packed up the notebook and her pen, but before she grabbed her bike, Jackie let out a whoop of joy to the sky. This was going to be the best year ever.

CHAPTER FIVE:
TERESA
YOU HAVE TO BE CAREFUL
ABOUT WHAT YOU WISH FOR

It was the longest week of Teresa's life. She had never been known to be a patient person, but now that she had to wait for her turn with actual magic, she thought she was going to lose her mind.

She tried to dream what her wish would be for the week, but her mind raced too fast for her to make a decision, and the thought of all of the opportunities made her palms sweat. She tried to distract herself with sports, but even though she was healed and the doctors declared her a miracle, her coach was still keeping her on the sidelines for most of the practices.

Coach Carter claimed she just wanted to be safe and make sure Teresa really was healed before they threw her out onto the field, but Teresa knew the real reason; it gave the other kids on the team the chance to play. Teresa knew she was a bit of a ball hog. Coaches had pulled her aside for this before, and her friends used to tease her about it all the time.

But she didn't understand. If you wanted to win, why wouldn't you let your best player do their thing? In the end, Teresa wanted to win, and she *knew* she was the best. She just knew it, and if she ever wanted to get anywhere in life, she needed to be able to prove herself on the field. Since her grades were a lost cause, there was no way she would ever get into college if she didn't get some sort of sport scholarship.

There was nothing Teresa could do but wait. Panic washed over her every minute that she wasted sitting on the bench. She knew that she was getting weaker and watching her team get stronger. She cared about her teammates, but she understood that they would eventually be her competition for positions on adult teams.

To make matters worse, the first day of seventh grade quickly closed in on them, and before Teresa knew it, she was back in that little corner classroom with the same obnoxious classmates as last year. Only this year, the girls rolled their eyes at everything the teacher said, and the boys had gotten taller and became even *more* annoying.

Teresa tapped her pencil on her desk, and thought about how much easier her life would be if she was smarter. She wouldn't have to stress as much about her future and she could get away from these obnoxious jerks and teachers who tapped their fingers on her desk because apparently, *she* was being distracting with her pencil jam out.

The whole week felt like it dragged on and on. Since Jackie wasn't allowed to make another wish, there had been very little to report from the group throughout the week at lunch.

On Monday, Jackie announced that she was determined to try to run for class president this year so she could make it a rule that every Friday was Pizza Friday in order to boost morale in the school.

On Tuesday, Sam told them through calling, wheedling, and probably money exchanging hands, her mom managed to get her into all of the highest classes. So even though it was the first week, Sam was already drowning in homework and miserable.

Kylie, other than being glasses-free, seemed like she was the same girl as always, which is something that Teresa always loved about Kylie. She was solid and reliable. When it seemed that the rest of the world was losing their minds, Kylie was always just chilling, being her normal self.

Then it was Friday. Blessed, magical Friday, but Teresa still had to wait, since the only class that all four girls had together was lunch.

When it was finally lunch, Teresa practically sprinted into the cafeteria and threw herself onto the bench next to Sam who always packed her lunch in an eco-friendly lunchbox. Sam gave her arm an excited squeeze before she unpacked her carrot sticks and organic hummus.

"Do you know what you're going to wish for?" Sam asked as she tossed her apple from hand to hand.

"I have like a million ideas; it's trying to pick one that's going to be the problem."

At last, Kylie and Jackie emerged from the lunch lines and hurried over to their table. With an air of ceremony, they placed their trays of square cardboard pizza on the table.

Even though it was still early September and smoldering hot in the cafeteria, Teresa noticed Jackie was wearing an oversized hoodie that bulged strangely around her stomach.

"Mr. Garrion is a tyrant, and I knew that he wouldn't let me bring the notebook into the cafeteria, so I had to make some tactical maneuvers," she explained

"Oooh, tactical. Someone has been working on their vocabulary words this week," Sam laughed.

"Cool. Can you give it to me?" Teresa didn't want to be rude, but her patience was hanging on by a thread.

Jackie pulled the notebook out from under her hoodie, and the other three girls held their breath as she handed it to Teresa.

Teresa ran her hand over the smooth leather and flipped through the yellowed pages. She glanced through Jackie's entry in the notebook, but since there was really nothing new to report, she didn't take a lot of time with it.

Also, she would never admit it, but Jackie had a habit of using really big words in her writing, so Teresa didn't always know what she was talking about.

Jackie pulled her purple pen out of her pocket and handed it to Teresa, "The power is in your hand."

Trembling, she took the pen out of Jackie's hand and tapped it on her lip. Meanwhile, the other three girls looked on breathlessly, waiting for Teresa to decide on her wish.

Though there were so many things that Teresa could choose from, there was one thing she knew she wanted more than anything else. So, with a flush rising up her neck, Teresa wrote large and clear into the notebook.

I wish that I was good at school.

The words began to fade, and the notebook began to glow, and the girls huddled over it so as to not draw attention.

"I had forgotten about the glowy thing," Teresa squeaked, looking over her shoulder. "Maybe next time, we should rethink the whole cafeteria thing."

"I agree. But, more importantly, Teresa, you don't need to wish for that." Kylie said sympathetically. But Teresa didn't want to hear it and besides, it was too late. The wish was already made.

"Guys, you're sweet, but let's be honest," Teresa spoke firmly, although she could feel the heat of embarrassment rising from her neck to her face, "I'm dumb. I always have been. I'm tired of not being in the same classes as any of you."

Jackie opened her mouth to argue, but Sam pulled on her sleeve to shush her.

"This isn't our choice to make. So if this is what you really want..." Sam sighed, "Though I can promise you that being really good at school isn't always what it's cracked up to be."

"It's done," Teresa sniffed, and Kylie wrapped her arms around her in a sympathetic hug.

"She's right," Jackie added, "The words are gone. There's no going back now."

"How do you feel?" Sam asked, cocking her head from side to side, "You don't look any different."

"Of course, she doesn't look different," Kylie laughed.

"I don't know," Sam cried defensively, "I thought she'd change and somehow look..."

"Smarter?" Teresa finished with a bitter grin, "Well, I guess that's not how it works. It's weird, though; I don't feel any different. There was something right away with my leg and Kylie's glasses."

"Maybe the notebook doesn't work with that kind of wish; maybe it needs to be a more physical thing," Kylie added.

Sam tapped her chin thoughtfully, while Jackie couldn't hide the disappointment that clouded her face.

The bell rang, and the girls snarfed down what they could of their lunches before they had to throw away their trays.

"Make sure to document *everything!*" Jackie cried as they were ushered back to their classes.

Teresa trudged along behind them, feeling defeated. It was her week for a wish, and she had wasted it. Now she would have to wait three more weeks until she had the chance to make up for her mistake.

It wasn't until she was halfway through her math class that Teresa realized she hadn't made a mistake. She hadn't made any mistake at all.

Before, the numbers of the worksheets always seemed to dance around the page, making no rhyme or reason to Teresa. Now, she flew through the equations. The answers sprang into her mind without a struggle. When the teacher wrote the terms for the day on the board, Teresa found she already knew what they meant without the teacher having to define them.

Teresa was so excited, when the teacher asked for a volunteer to complete a problem on the Smartboard, Teresa actually raised her hand *and volunteered.* She never volunteered in class if she could help it. Not no way, not no how.

Now, she was twirling the pen in her hand and confidently scribbling down numbers like they were no big deal.

It wasn't just math, though. In reading, the words that usually mushed together or appeared backward to her now lined up neatly for Teresa like soldiers in a line. She couldn't just read the words; she could *understand them.* The whole idea of 'reading comprehension' her Special Education case manager was always babbling to her about finally started to make sense. Teresa felt like she had finally unlocked a secret code that had been hidden away from her for years.

By the end of the day, Teresa was on cloud nine. All of her homework was already done, and she was confident it was all correct.

Her parents were going to be so proud of her when they saw how her grades were going to grow. It was only going to be a matter of time before she was moved out of the no man's land classroom and put in with her friends.

Teresa didn't care if she wasn't put into the high classes with Sam and Jackie. If she could at least be in Kylie's classes she would be happy. Not only would she finally have a friend to talk with, but she wouldn't be an outcast anymore. When the girls worked on their homework together at lunch, Teresa wouldn't have to feel embarrassed to show them her worksheets, which were always shorter in length and in a strangely large print. It was like the teachers thought if the letters were bigger, then, somehow, they would better sink into their thick skulls.

Nope, she wouldn't have to lie and say she didn't have any homework that day to avoid the humiliating comments her friends would make.

They never meant harm, she knew this, but when

Sam would mention how she had learned to do the equations on Teresa's papers "years ago," or when Jackie's pen would turn her essays from black and white to rainbow with all the corrections she made, Teresa wanted to die.

Not this year. This year was going to be different, and the best part was it was only just the beginning. There were still so many wishes she could make.

Teresa hummed to herself as she laced up her cleats for soccer practice that afternoon. She was so lost in her thoughts that she didn't notice at first that her cleats seemed a bit tighter than usual, and when she stood up a sharp twinge of pain shot up her ankle. But she paid it no mind, figuring that it was probably some aftermath from when she sprained her ankle. She was sure that once she had warmed up and stretched a bit, she would be fine.

What she didn't expect was when her teammate kicked the ball at her, she would kick it back, only for an unbelievable pain to shoot up her leg, making her scream and crumple to the ground.

CHAPTER SIX:
SAM
APPLES ARE THEIR OWN KIND
OF MAGIC

S am loved apples. She didn't really love them as something to eat. As far as fruit went taste-wise, apples were perfectly fine, but nothing to write home about. But drawing apples. That was absolute magic. At the beginning of class, the art teacher, Mrs. Bringston, brought out a bundle of fruits and told them to pick one and create a still life surrounding it.

Most of the other kids in the class groaned. They wanted to draw anime characters or make clay figures because that was the messiest medium to work with, but Sam had to hold herself back from clapping her hands together.

She loved still life. She adored examining the ordinary and finding the beautiful nuances that most people don't take the time to see.

For example, when most people think about apples, they imagine the color red. But that wasn't true. Yes, there are yellow and green apples. But even your average 'red' apple really wasn't just red. The basic apple in front of Sam had shades of red to it, but there was also golden yellow and white mixed with dark browns and deep purples. Even the stem had tinges of green. Even more to the apple was the texture. There was a smoothness to a good apple that made it gleam and shine in the sunlight, and tempted one to take a bite of it.

Between her own musings, the sound of classical music, and the smell of acrylics, Sam had lost all track of time and her surroundings. When the bell rang for her next class, she was so startled she almost fell off of her seat.

"Alright, boys and girls, please make sure your name is on the back of your papers and put them on the third shelf so that they don't get lost."

Sam sighed and began packing up her things, but before she left, Mrs. Bringston gently tapped her on the shoulder.

"I just wanted to let you know, Sam, that we'll be starting the Art Academics in a few weeks. There is still time for you to give me a submission if you're interested."

Sam's heart ached. The Art Academics was an after-school class you had to apply to get into. Only the best artists in the school were accepted, and it was a great opportunity for students to improve their artistic work. Mrs. Bringston had recommended Sam for the class last year, and though Sam had begged her mom to let her at least apply, she had refused.

Sam couldn't bring herself to look at Mrs. Bringston as she muttered her reply. "I'd love to, Mrs. Bringston. I really would, but you know my mom...."

Mrs. Bringston nodded her head. There was no more that needed to be said. Sam's mom was infamous amongst the faculty as being a 'difficult' parent. "I completely understand, Sam, and I don't want to pressure you," Mrs. Bringston gently placed a piece of paper into Sam's hand, "but I just want you to know your options."

Sam was so upset she could barely mutter out a "thank you" before she rushed to her next class. Later on, she could barely listen to her English teacher drone on and on about text-dependent analysis essays. She was too busy trying to hide the tears sliding down her nose. She knew she was being dramatic. She had great friends, a nice house, parents who cared about her, and a bunch of other great things in her life.

But it didn't feel like *her* life. Sam felt like everyone else was in control, and she was just a pawn being moved around a chessboard. She was so tired of doing what other people told her to do. She wanted to do what *she* wanted to do, eat what she wanted to eat, and wear whatever she wanted to wear. Why couldn't her mother take up yoga and become one of those hippy-dippy free-range mothers who never assigned curfews and served ice cream for dinner, or at least let her apply for the Art Academics. But Sam knew that it would never happen in a million years.

Sam sulked for the rest of the day. She walked through the halls like she was trudging through thick mud and her head was heavy and fuzzy.

On the bus ride home, she didn't feel like talking to anyone, and thankfully, her seatmate Kylie picked up on Sam's mood and didn't pry into what was wrong. She just let Sam put her Air Pods in and lean her head against the cool bus window.

When Sam got home, she threw her backpack by the door, not caring about the mountains of homework she had to get done or the fact that her mom was going to scold her for leaving her things around the house. All she could think about was getting to her bed as quickly as possible and burying herself under the covers.

Once she was neatly tucked under her sky-blue comforter, she put her Air Pods back into her ears and was just about to drift off to sleep when her phone absolutely exploded with texts. She grabbed her phone and saw that it was a mixture of texts from Jackie and Kylie about Teresa being back in the ER.

Confused and worried, Sam threw her sheets to the side and sat up. Teresa had the notebook. How could this have happened? Did she make a wish that backfired, or

41

maybe this was just a terrible coincidence?

The girls texted each other frantically, but Teresa wasn't responding to any of their messages which made everything a thousand times more frightening.

Sam was so nervous about Teresa that afternoon that during Mandarin class she misspelled several words on her worksheet, and her tutor had to remind her several times to pay attention.

Then when her mom got home, she scolded Sam about her backpack sprawled on the ground, but she didn't even flinch. During dinner, her mind was so clouded with worry that she broke two dishes and a cup. She must have appeared pretty upset because her mother actually placed a tender hand on her forehead instead of scolding her for her clumsiness.

"Sammie, hun, are you feeling alright?" her mother asked with what sounded like actual concern.

"Yeah..." Sam began hesitantly. "Teresa got hurt again, and I haven't heard anything from her, so I guess I'm just worried if she's ok."

Sam was surprised the words actually tumbled out of her mouth. She couldn't remember the last time she had said a word to her mom about her personal life, let alone a whole sentence.

Her mother tutted and pulled Sam in for a hug, and Sam breathed in the familiar, light, clean scent of her mother's perfume, "Aw honey, I'm sorry to hear that. Maybe Teresa is sleeping, or they're still at the doctors', and she can't get ahold of her phone. Do you want me to call her mom and see how everything's going?"

Why was her mother being so nice all of a sudden? Did her mother want something from her? Did she do something like read her journal again? No, that didn't make sense. She wouldn't feel bad about that. Maybe she was possessed or was some sort of changeling. Sam had read stories about fairies who snatched babies away and replaced them with evil fairy look-alikes.

No, her mom was way too old to be taken by a fairy, and besides, knowing her mother, she would probably slap the fairy away with her purse before it even got the chance to lay a finger on her. Either way, her mom's offer was well-meaning, so Sam allowed herself to sink against her mom's chest and shook her head.

"No," she mumbled, "I don't want to bother them if it's something really serious."

As her mom tucked her hair behind her ear, Sam noticed that if she was standing upright, she'd almost be as tall as her mom. She also realized that beneath her mom's power suits, she was actually quite small and frail. Growing up, Sam's mom had always seemed so huge to her. She was like some thundering giant that took up the entire room. When had she gotten so tiny?

Eventually, her mom pulled away, breaking the magic, and patted her on the head, "Well, I'm sure everything is going to be just fine. You'll probably hear from her in the morning, though I'm honestly not surprised to hear that she's been hurt again. She's a nice girl, but she's always been a bit... rough around the edges if you know what I mean?"

Just like that, the tenderness Sam felt towards her mother evaporated, and she stepped backward, folding her arms across her chest. "Mmmm..." Sam grunted, not wanting to give her mother any more opportunity to pick apart her friends. "Well, thanks, Mom, but I better get going. I have English homework that I have to get done."

"Do you need any help?" Sam's mom asked, neatly folding the dish towel away, "You can bring it into the kitchen, I can make some tea, and we can work on it together. We used to do all of your projects like that."

Yeah, Sam thought bitterly, *and you would breathe down my neck the entire time.*

Sam grabbed her backpack and moved back toward the door as if she was trying to escape one of the dinosaurs from Jurassic Park, "Uh, thanks, Mom, but I really do concentrate better in my room."

"Oh, alright, if you say so. But you better actually be working in there and not just listening to your music and staring at your phone."

"Yup!" Sam squeaked as she scurried away, desperate to avoid the disappointed look on her mother's face.

Once she was back in her room, Sam threw her backpack next to her desk, then flung herself onto her bed. She wasn't lying when she said she had English homework, but there was no way any of it was going to get done tonight. Instead, she reached for her phone, which she had to keep in her room during dinner since phones were not allowed at the table, and she gasped when she saw that Teresa had finally texted back.

> *Teresa-*
> *Ankle's re-sprained. We need to have a Winsome Foursome meeting STAT. I've learned something about the notebook, and things are not as simple as we thought they were.*

Sam pulled the covers up to her chin and bit her nail. First of all, she was deeply impressed by Teresa's improved spelling. Sam would never tell her this because she didn't want to seem like a snob or hurt Teresa's feelings, but there were times when Teresa's spelling was so bad she honestly had no idea what she was trying to text, and she would have to wait for Jackie to decipher the message for her.

But what got Sam's heart pounding was the fact that this injury could somehow have been caused by the notebook. Jackie's earlier warning danced in Sam's head, and she couldn't help but now worry that they had released some sort of evil magic onto the world and Derrison Middle School.

Clutching her phone to her chest, Sam lay wide-eyed in her bed. There was no way she was going to get any sleep tonight. I mean, what if she and her friends had unleashed a monster?!

Please don't be a giant snake, Sam prayed. *I really, really hate snakes.*

CHAPTER SEVEN:
KYLIE
LIFE IS LEARNING TO ADJUST

That night, Kylie's heart ached for Teresa. Even though she knew things could be much worse, Kylie understood how important sports were to her. So, when she realized that Teresa had the opportunity to play ripped away from her yet again, she felt like she could cry.

Lunch the next day was a solemn affair. Jackie and Kylie placed their lunches down quietly, as Sam picked at her apple slices. There was none of Jackie's normal excited chatter. There weren't Sam's usual offers to trade her vegetables for her guilty pleasure of spicy Cheetos.

Instead, the lunch room had become a room where they waited for Teresa to hobble over to them on her crutches. After an uncomfortably long time, she awkwardly sank herself into the seat, and the silence was broken by a frantic interrogation from Sam and Jackie. Kylie, as usual, leaned back and listened to the conversation unfold.

"Oh, my God! What happened?"

"What did you do with the notebook, you nutcase?!"

Teresa waved a hashbrown, silencing them. Once she was sure that she had their full attention, she launched into her story. She explained how the wish had worked. How school suddenly seemed like a breeze in the blink of an eye.

"But then..." Teresa said, shaking her head, "Everything got even weirder. My ankle started acting up again, and as soon as I touched a soccer ball, I was on the ground in even worse pain than before."

"Did you kick the ball in a weird way and maybe injure yourself again? What did the doctor say?" Sam, who always tried to find the logical explanation, asked.

"No way. My foot barely touched the ball," Teresa replied, "And the doctors said it was the strangest thing that they have ever seen. They insist it's sprained again, but they want me to come back again today so that they can do more tests. My mom is freaking out. She doesn't know who she wants to yell at more, the doctors or me."

"You think the notebook had something to do with this." Jackie pressed.

"Uh, yeah..." Teresa answered bluntly, "I thought about it all last night, and the only conclusion that I could come up with is that the notebook has its own set of rules, and one of them is that it only allows one wish per person. Once you make another wish, the first wish stops working. I mean, think about it, I wished to be healed and I was feeling great, but as soon as I wished for something else, I was suddenly in the EXACT same pain as I was before. That's no coincidence."

"Whenever you make a new wish..." Jackie muttered.

"It cancels out the wish from before..." Sam finished.

"Whatever you wish for really should be for just that week," Jackie remarked, waving one of Sam's carrot sticks in the air.

"Or you just make the one wish, and that's it," Sam added, grabbing one of Jackie's nuggets off her tray.

"Do you think there could be a loophole to the rule? Like wishing for more wishes?" Jackie asked.

Teresa shrugged, "I have no idea. But I'm done. I'll write down if anything else happens to me during the week, but I'm not going to be the guinea pig any more. Sam, you're next, so you can be the one who plays around with it."

Sam pushed the notebook right over to Kylie.

"I'm not ready yet. I need my wish to be just perfect and I can't think on the spot like this."

Kylie rubbed her eyes. It was so like Sam to freak out like this. Kylie would never tell Sam this, but even though Sam tried to act like she was nothing like her mom, the two of them were identical perfectionists.

Sighing, Kylie traced the rim of her nose. She had gotten used to not having to wear her glasses, but she figured it wouldn't be the worst thing in the world if she had to start wearing them again, especially if she got the chance for a more exciting wish. But there were so many options, and her friends were relying on her now. She didn't want to make a mistake and ruin the notebook for the rest of them.

"What should I say when I get the notebook?" Kylie asked the group nervously. This was now the second time she had been put on the spot.

"Well, that depends on what you want to wish for," Jackie replied.

"I don't even know yet," Kylie replied honestly.

"Well, whatever you wish for, you're going to have to be very careful about the wording," Sam interjected. "Do you think you can double up on a wish, like do I wish for a cat *and* a dog?"

"I think someone is going to have to wish for infinite wishes," Jackie insisted.

Teresa and Kylie watched silently as Sam and Jackie volleyed back and forth with ideas.

Kylie was about to joke to Teresa that watching Jackie and Sam debate was like watching a never-ending tennis game, but she saw the quiet look of sadness on Teresa's face, and the words disappeared in her mouth.

"Hey," Kylie whispered to Teresa, "Why don't I wish for your ankle to be healed? Then you could play soccer again."

Teresa smiled but shook her head, "That's really

sweet, Kylie, but that's not fair to you. Besides, I already made a wish about my ankle. I feel like if I do it again, I'm going to do some freaky damage to my leg, and my mom's head will explode from confusion. Also, I don't want doctors to take me away to some secret lab to experiment on me because they think I'm like an X-Men mutant or something."

"But what about soccer season?" Kylie asked gently.

"There will be others," Teresa sighed, and Kylie wrapped her arm around her friend's shoulder with a reassuring squeeze.

"We've come to an agreement!"

Kylie and Teresa jumped in surprise.

"I know we just started, but I think we need to make an exception to the rules so we can feel the magic out." Jackie declared, wild-eyed.

Sam continued, "Teresa, we want to leave it up to you since you are the one who has experienced... damage because of the notebook. Would you rather make another wish, or are you ok with just giving the notebook to Kylie now, so we can see what happens when she makes a wish?"

Teresa threw her hands up in the air, "If you don't want it, Sam, give it to Kylie. Seriously. I think I need a break from the notebook for a little bit."

Kylie blinked with bewilderment, "Uh, yeah. That's fine with me. What do you guys want me to do?"

The bell rang, signaling the end of lunch and making the four girls groan in frustration. Jackie grabbed Kylie by the arm, talking a mile a minute as the rest of the grade threw out the trash on their trays and started to file out of the door, "You need to make a wish. Something small, and you need to see if you need your glasses again."

"But try and play with the wording and see if you can find a workaround!" Sam added.

Kylie turned to Teresa, but she had already hobbled her way out of the cafeteria.

"We need to understand how this works," Jackie insisted as she shoved the notebook against Kylie's chest.

Kylie gaped, trying to think of something to say, but it was too late. Sam and Jackie were already hurrying away to class. Nervously, Kylie wrapped her arms around the cool leather and made her way to science class, completely unsure of what she should do next.

The late bell rang just as Kylie stepped into the lab. Mr. Becks raised his eyebrows at her but didn't say anything as she settled herself into her lab table.

With shaking hands, Kylie shoved the notebook into her backpack and chewed on the end of her pencil. Kylie had trouble making decisions. She thought over every option carefully, weighing her wants against what would be best for her and most importantly, wouldn't hurt other people's feelings.

This meant it took her a painfully long time to choose something, which drove her siblings nuts. Shopping with Kylie could take hours as she toiled over what color shirt to buy, and on the rare times that her family went out to eat, Kylie would freeze, taking in all the options, and end up panicking and ordering the chicken fingers, which is what she always ended up with at every restaurant, whether she liked it or not.

The truth was, Kylie didn't actually make a lot of decisions in her life. Usually, her self-assured siblings would get impatient with her and end up making choices for her, which always bothered her. Kylie knew what she wanted, it just took her a while to figure out exactly what that was, and it sucked that she always had to be rushed or crushed under the avalanche of louder voices/

But now, it was her responsibility to make a wish. And not just any wish, but one that would test the very foundations of some unknown magic they had discovered. It was a wish that could make her life incredible or ruin her forever! There were countless possibilities and ways this could all go wrong! Oh God, why didn't she just ask Sam or Jackie what they wanted her to wish for? They were the smart ones.

"Kylie, can you tell us the answer to number five?"

Mr. Becks' low voice broke Kylie out of her concentration, and she stared dumbfounded at the periodic element she was supposed to identify on the board.

"Uh... it's uh..."

"Calcium. It's calcium," came a whisper from across the lab table.

"Calcium!" Kylie declared.

Mr. Becks raised his eyebrows and shook his head slightly, "That is correct. I do ask next time, James, you let Kylie figure it out on her own."

The class chuckled, and Kylie felt her face redden as Mr. Becks went on to go over the other answers to the worksheet that they were supposed to be working on.

"Thanks..." Kylie muttered to James, unable to look him in the eye.

James didn't respond, and Kylie wondered with terror if he was mad at her now.

James had been in all of Kylie's classes since they were in fourth grade, and Kylie had a crush on him since fifth grade. Jackie and Teresa had been pushing her to try and talk to him for years, but whenever Kylie looked too long at his swoopy blonde hair, and freckle-covered nose, her tongue felt like it swelled up, and all she could ever choke out was a one-word answer here or there.

Her older sister Clara would have known what to say. Boys always liked Clara and they had followed her around like puppies for as long as Kylie could remember. Then Kylie would watch in awe as Clara sassed them away or rolled her eyes at their jokes.

She didn't care about the attention she was getting. Clara was going to do whatever she wanted to do.

Kylie couldn't relate.

On the one hand, Kylie was fascinated with boys and wanted a boyfriend more than anything else, but on the other hand, they were a mystery to her. Kylie had brothers. But they were her stupid, smelly siblings. They were different from *actual* boys like James.

Part of the reason why Kylie wished to not have glasses anymore was secretly in hopes that James would notice and say something. However, even though he was right across from her, he didn't seem to notice the change, and they had only exchanged a handful of words with each other so far this year.

Sighing, Kylie absentmindedly doodled a flower on the corner of her worksheet when a light bulb suddenly went off inside her. An actual decision was starting to take form in her mind, and Kylie realized she knew what she wanted to wish for.

Chapter Eight:
Jackie
Magic is More Complicated
Than We Thought

"Yeah. I see what you're saying, but I think you're missing a key element of who Ponyboy is as a person! If you don't see what I'm saying, then you don't have any idea of who Ponyboy is as a character at all, and we are really going to need to relook at this assignment."

Jackie's reading group blinked back at her with frightened confusion. They were supposed to discuss the characterization of different characters from *The Outsiders*. Jackie's group had been assigned Ponyboy, and it seemed very apparent to Jackie that she was the only one who had done the reading.

Miss Sniver gently tapped Jackie on the shoulder. "We've talked about this, Jackie. I love how... enthusiastic you are about our readings, but you have to be respectful of your classmates and their answers."

"But, Miss Sniver..." Jackie began to whine. But Miss Sniver gave her one of those teacher looks. You know, one of those expressions that somehow every teacher has managed to learn that tells you "Shut up right now, or I'm going to have to raise my voice" without ever saying a word.

Jackie clamped her mouth shut, and Miss Sniver gave her a nod of approval before turning to the rest of her group.

"Now, Ben, why don't you tell me some things that come to your mind when you think of Ponyboy as a character."

"Uhhhhhh...." Ben drew out. Jackie swore she could practically see smoke come out of his ears as he tried to think. "He's nice."

"Ok," Miss Sniver responded gently, "Why do you think he's nice? What evidence from the book gives you the idea that he's nice?"

"He... uh... is nice to his friends?" Ben blurted out and grinned moronically at his friends, who laughed behind him.

As Miss Sniver continued trying to press Ben for an actual useful thought, Jackie rolled her eyes.

Normally, Jackie loved Reading. It was her favorite class. But today, she didn't have any patience for Miss Sniver who, to be honest, was sweet but kind of a doormat, and her classmates who didn't care about anything other than the latest TikTok.

Jackie wanted to scream. *Don't you realize that there is so much more to the world?! There is magic! Real-life actual freaking magic! That's what we should be trying to figure out right now!*

But there was nothing that she could do. Kylie was the one with the notebook right now, and knowing Kylie, she was not going to decide on her wish any time soon. That didn't mean Jackie's mind wasn't constantly on the notebook, though. She still couldn't believe it was real. All her life, Jackie had wanted magic to be real. She had read every fantasy book she could get her hands on and had played make-believe much longer than any of her friends.

She would never admit this out loud, even under the threat of death, but part of her still even believed in Santa. She knew that it was her parents buying the gifts. She wasn't crazy! But the idea and special feeling she got thinking about Santa was something she couldn't bear to lose. So, starting last year, Jackie started collecting Santas. Santa figurines, Santa stuffed animals, Santa pictures, and ornaments; If Santa's face was on it, Jackie bought it, bartered for it, or was gifted it. She then kept them all in a red chest under her bed.

But the discovery of the notebook was better than any Santa collectible. Honestly, Jackie didn't even need to make any more wishes. This was the greatest thing she could wish for. But Jackie liked to understand, she liked to learn, and now this notebook was an experiment and puzzle that she wanted to get her hands on.

Class ended, and she was freed from Miss Sniver's pained expression as she tried to pull any logical thought out of Ben Robert's bird brain.

As she made her way to the gym, Jackie snuck a peek at her phone, and a slow grin spread across her face as she read Kylie's text.

Kylie-
Got an idea for wish. Dont want to make it alone thou. Can we meet up sumtime 2day?

Heart pounding, Jackie texted her mom and friends as rapidly as possible. She was so excited she didn't listen as the gym teacher described the rules of the game they were playing that day. She didn't care that her overly competitive classmates were screaming at her to run, or when a kickball flew in the air and smacked her in the back of the head.

By the end of the day, everyone was able to work out their schedules and talk to their parents. Well, in Sam's case, she more lied to her parent, but desperate times call for desperate actions. It was agreed that they would meet at Teresa's house for a 'study' session.

The hours seemed to drag by as Jackie pondered over what Kylie was going to wish for and what was going to happen after she made it. At last, it was time, and Jackie practically threw herself out of her mom's car and ran to Teresa's door.

Teresa's mom answered, and Jackie had to politely swallow her impatience as she offered her drinks and snacks. After reassuring her that she was well-fed and hydrated, Jackie joined Sam, who was sitting cross-legged on the floor munching on some popcorn, and Teresa, who had her leg propped up on the couch.

"Kylie's not here yet?" Jackie sighed with exasperation.

"You know how her mom is," Teresa answered as she tried to catch a kernel of popcorn that Sam was aiming at her mouth.

With so many siblings and only two cars, Kylie's parents were notorious for being late since they usually had to make multiple stops.

With a huff, Jackie plunked herself on the couch, her leg jiggling with impatience.

Thankfully, she didn't have to wait long before the doorbell rang, and the three girls rushed to answer the door.

They practically dragged Kylie to the living room, and after a few more reassurances to Teresa's mom that they had enough food and drinks, they began the interrogation.

"What are you going to wish for?" Jackie blurted out immediately.

Kylie looked down at her lap and picked at her nails nervously. "Ok, first of all, I need you all to promise me that you're not going to freak out or judge me or anything."

"Kylie, we're your friends. We would never make fun of you," Teresa reassured her.

"Well..." Kylie began, her face growing redder and redder with every second, "Do you guys know James from my science class?"

"Yes..." The girls responded in unison, and Jackie's heart started to pound with excitement as realization began to dawn on her.

"Well, You guys know that I've always kinda...

sorta... thought he was cute," Kylie continued. Jackie could have sworn that if Kylie's face had gotten any brighter her head was going to pop right off of her shoulders.

Teresa and Jackie squealed so loud that Teresa's mom peeked her head into the living room, probably because she was concerned that her daughter had sprained another body part.

The comments poured out in a whirlwind of glee.

"Have you talked to him?"

"Has he gotten any taller?"

"Oh my God, you two are going to be so cute. Can I be one of your bridesmaids when you guys get married?"

It was Sam, ever the practical one, who brought them back to why they were at Teresa's house in the first place.

"Yeah, he seems nice, I guess... But what does this have to do with your wish?"

"Well," Kylie pulled the notebook gently out of her backpack and placed it sheepishly on the couch, "I was kinda hoping that we could use the notebook to get James to like me?"

CHAPTER NINE:
TERESA
DRAMA TRUMPS ALL

Teresa wanted to hop up and down, but since that wasn't possible with her ankle, she chose to clap her hands instead.

Was this the best use of the notebook? Probably not. Could this unlock a whole treasure trove of issues? Most likely. Did Teresa care? Not really. Even though she was a self-described jock, Teresa was a total sucker for romance. None of the foursome had even had a boyfriend, unless you counted the three-hour time period in fourth grade when Jackie was apparently 'dating' Trey Robinson, even though they never actually spoke to each other.

But Kylie was always such a people pleaser, it was nice to see her wanting something just for herself.

"Kylie, I'm excited for you, I really am," Sam began carefully, "But I feel like there's a lot of ways this could go wrong. Like, would you really be happy knowing that he only liked you because of magic?"

"Sam!" Teresa scolded.

But Jackie bit down on a chip thoughtfully, "She does have a point. But I'm more concerned with the notebook specifics here. I mean, based on what Teresa says, if you make another wish, it cancels out the last wish you made. So, if you want to use your wish to get James to like you, then you really can't make any other wishes unless you don't care about him not liking you anymore."

Kylie played with a lock of her hair, and Teresa could see that she was trying to hide the tears that were starting to well up in her eyes.

"Yeah..." Kylie said softly, "I guess I wasn't thinking. Sorry guys, it was a stupid idea."

"It wasn't a stupid idea at all," Teresa replied, glaring at Sam and Jackie.

"No! It was a great idea!" Jackie added quickly.

"I just think that if we're testing out magic, we maybe shouldn't start with something so... emotional," Sam added, looking unsure.

"You're in Mr. Becks' class, right? I heard he does a biosphere partner project for most of the year, and you have to spend a TON of time with your partner. Maybe you can wish for Mr. Becks to put you two together?"

"That's a great idea!" Teresa cried enthusiastically.

Kylie asked for so little and was usually overshadowed by her siblings. Teresa was desperate for her to have something that was just for her.

Kylie bit down on the end of her hair, her head furrowed in concentration. Finally, she gave a slight nod and smiled slightly.

"Mr. Becks was saying just the other day that we were to start our partner project tomorrow. I wouldn't even have to wait long. I just want to get to know him a bit more and maybe even stand out to him a little."

Teresa clapped when Kylie flipped open the notebook, and Jackie passed her the pen with ceremonious seriousness.

"You two are going to be so cute together!" Teresa squeaked.

"Wait, though," Jackie interrupted, "How are we going to word this? We want to see if there's a way that you don't lose your first wish."

"Maybe you can do an and situation. Like I wish that Mr. Becks would pair us together AND that I can keep my eyesight."

"That's not a bad idea," Jackie added, "But it almost feels too easy. Maybe try something a bit more formal, like, ``With my eyes still free of glasses, I wish that Mr. Becks would pair James and me together."

"Oh, that sounds really cool," Teresa whispered. Jackie was a wizard with words.

"But doesn't that leave room open for interpretation?" Sam asked, "Like it could be taken as I have my eyesight now, but that doesn't mean it'll let you keep your wish for the future."

Sam and Jackie continued back and forth until Teresa couldn't take it anymore, and she let out a loud, "Stop!"

Jackie and Sam jumped back and stared at Teresa wide-eyed.

"It's Kylie's wish. Let her make the wish however she wants."

"No, Teresa. It's fine. I wouldn't know what to say anyway," Kylie argued

But a shamefaced Jackie and Sam were already apologizing to her, and Kylie knew that it was too late for her to try and change their minds.

Kylie played with the pen and considered all of her options. Teresa was right. This was her wish, and darn it, she was going to take her time making it.

Kylie stared at the page for what felt like hours. Realistically, Teresa knew that it was probably only a few minutes, but it was long enough that the other three girls actually started to lose interest in what she was going to wish for and turned their attention to the teen girl reality show that was blasting in the background.

Just as Teresa and Jackie were starting to debate the merits of night showers over day showers, Sam suddenly shushed them and pointed at Kylie, who was carefully scribbling away in the notebook.

Breathless, they waited for Kylie to finish and placed the pen on the table. The notebook glowed, sending a soft light around Teresa's living room, and then just as quickly as the words had appeared, they were gone.

"What did you end up wishing for?" Teresa whispered. Her mom was upstairs in her room, and the girls had been talking at a regular volume until this moment, but now Teresa had the same feeling she got when her mom dragged her to church.

"More importantly, what were the exact words that you used?" Sam scrunched up her brow the same way she did when trying to figure out a particularly difficult homework assignment.

"Well, I went with the partner idea. I thought that wouldn't be asking too much," Kylie responded shyly, "but I worded it the way that Jackie said because I liked the way that it sounded."

Jackie grinned, and Sam let out a small sigh, "Drama trumps all, as always."

Jackie elbowed Sam in the ribs. "Hush,"

Teresa waved her hand in front of Kylie's face, "Can you see? How many fingers am I holding up?

Kylie giggled, "Yes, I can see, and you're holding up three fingers."

"It worked!" Jackie cheered, but Sam looked less convinced.

"It may only be working now because the wish hasn't actually begun yet." Sam added, but when she saw the look of disappointment on Kylie's face, she waved her hands back and forth, "But I could totally be wrong."

"We'll just have to wait and see," Teresa added thoughtfully, and the girls gathered together for a group hug.

As the night wore on, the atmosphere started to calm, and the girls started to talk about familiar things, though there were a lot more giggles whenever they talked to Kylie.

But soon time slipped away, and Jackie, Sam, and Kylie were all picked up by their parents, and Teresa was left with nothing but her thoughts.

Teresa found that ever since she made her wish in the notebook, her thoughts flowed together more smoothly. Before, Teresa always felt like her mind was a mishmash of strings that tangled up together and jumped from one idea to the next, and the only time she ever felt really focused was when she was on the sports field.

But now, she felt like her brain was like a rock-less river that moved easily from one spot to another. On one hand, this was a great relief, and Teresa found that she was having an easier time falling asleep without her random ideas and song lyrics popping into her head, but there was a little part of her that missed her old brain, even though she couldn't exactly put a finger on why.

That night, as Teresa lay in bed, she closed her eyes and tried to allow her mind absolute freedom. But in return, all she received was calm silence. It was then that she realized what she missed about her old way of thinking. Now her mind was too quiet. It was almost eerie. Despite how annoying it used to be not being able to fall asleep, Teresa missed the noise. She missed the noise very much.

Chapter Ten:
Sam
There is Nothing Scarier
Than a Preteen Scorned

Sam's nails were bitten down to the skin by the time her mom and she had gotten home from Teresa's. It was a terrible habit, but she couldn't help it, especially when she was nervous, and right now she was definitely freaking out.

The parental consent for the Art Academics was due in three days. Sam knew that she should have asked sooner, but every time she thought she had worked up the courage to say something to her mom, her throat felt like it was going to close up, and her tongue felt like it was swelling in her mouth.

Her mom wasn't a monster. Sam knew that. She knew that her mother loved her very much, but she knew that her mom was most likely going to tell her no, and Sam didn't think her heart could bear the disappointment of not being able to follow her passion yet again.

Hesitantly, Sam followed her mom through the front door, her mom was chatting away about her latest client and how well her case had gone. Once they got inside, Sam's mom turned and gave her a great big smile, "How about a little ice cream before bed tonight? It'll be just a little celebratory treat, and besides, it's just vanilla, so it's not that terrible, right sweetheart?"

Sam picked at the skin of her thumbnail and smiled. Her mom was in such a good mood, and everything was going too well right now. Sam was tempted just to throw away the form and pretend like nothing was amiss. I mean, she could always try next year, right?

But as her mom scooped the ice cream carefully into two matching bowls, Sam knew that she would not get a better opportunity to talk to her mom than right now. She closed her eyes, wishing desperately it was her turn with the notebook so she could just wish this issue away.

But she was not so lucky. With a final deep breath, she thanked her mom for the ice cream, placed it on the table, and then with trembling hands, pulled the permission form out of her backpack.

"Hey, Mom..." she began.

Her mom took a big bite of ice cream and looked at her expectedly.

"There's this club at school that I really, really want to join. It shouldn't interfere with Mandarin or my other activities, and it'll make me look really well-rounded on my college applications, and it'll also make me so happy, and I promise if you let me do this, I'll never ask for anything ever again."

The words poured out of her in a nervous jumble, and when her request was met with silence, Sam worried that her mother didn't even understand what she was asking.

But to her surprise, her mother swallowed her ice cream and reached her hand out toward Sam. "Let me see," was all her mother said.

Sam handed the permission form to her mother. It took an eternity for her to read over the paper, and even though she was trying her best to appear patient and mature, Sam couldn't help herself from tapping her foot and gnawing on her nail as she waited.

Finally, her mom looked up at her, her mouth drawn into a straight line. She only said a single word, but it was enough to make Sam feel as if she had been slapped in the face.

"No."

Sam exhaled as if she had been punched in the gut.

"But whyyyyyyyyyyyyy?!" Sam knew she was whining. She also knew that her mother hated it when she whined, but at that moment, she didn't care what her mother thought. She was too busy trying to fight back the tears that were threatening to spill down her cheeks.

"Honey..." Sam's mom began. She spoke slowly as if she were talking to a three-year-old, or someone who couldn't hear very well, "I know you like to doodle, and I think it's a nice little hobby for when you have some free time. But you're starting to get to the age where you must take your school career seriously. Colleges aren't going to want to see that you took some silly little art class. They want to see that your extracurricular activities actually apply to the major you're going for.

"But it'll show that I have a variety of interests," Sam pleaded, "It'll help me stand out against all the other applicants. Isn't that what you told me I needed?"

Sam's mom smiled, which made Sam even angrier. "I see what you're saying, honey, but what I meant by that is they want to see people who have created new technological devices or have received great honors. A middle school art class isn't exactly what I meant."

"But it can't hurt," Sam added. But her mother just shook her head.

"I'm just looking out for your best interests, honey. After your test scores last year, I think the most important thing for you to do this year is to focus on your studies. With everything else you have going on, I'm afraid one more extracurricular activity might be too much, especially since you always want to spend so much time with your friends..." she added with a pointed look. "Now, if it was a math tutoring class, I might consider it since that would help boost your test grades to where they should be. But I'm sorry, honey, I think this would just be a waste of time."

"It wouldn't be a waste of time to me," Sam whined, stomping her feet. When planning this moment, Sam wanted to appear calm and mature, as if she and her mom were two adults having a business conference. But instead of feeling thirty-five, Sam felt like she had been thrown back in time to being five again. She was embarrassed at herself for acting this way, but even more, she was furious at her mother for making her feel this way.

"Sweetheart," her mom placed her spoon carefully on the table and reached out to brush the hair out of Sam's face, but instinctively, Sam pulled away, "I know you don't believe me right now, but trust me. This is in your best interest."

"How can it be in my best interest if it's not what I want? You never listen to me! You don't care at all about me. All you care about is making sure that I do what you say so that I don't embarrass you in front of your church friends. It doesn't matter how I feel, you just want a perfect little robot, and I hate you for it! I hate you so much, and I always will!" Sam screamed. Before her mother could respond, she sprinted to her room, slamming the door behind her. She grabbed her desk chair and propped it under the doorknob, and with dramatic gusto, threw herself onto the bed and cried into her pillow so hard hot spittle flew out of her mouth with the animal-like whimpers she made.

Sam's door rattled, and she could hear her mom calling from her from the other side, but she ignored her and clutched her pillow to her chest. At first, her mom called to her gently, but as time went on, she was clearly getting frustrated with Sam's actions, and she began pounding on the door. "Sam! You are being absolutely ridiculous! If you do not unlock this door right now, you are grounded until Thanksgiving break!"

She knew that her mom wasn't bluffing, but Sam

didn't want to give her the satisfaction of seeing her open the door with her tail between her legs. If punishment was what it took for Sam to make her grandstand, then it was going to be worth it.

On the other side of the door, Sam's mom let out an aggravated huff, "That's it, Samantha! You are grounded! And if you aren't downstairs tomorrow for breakfast at 7:30 sharp, so help me, I will break this door down!" With a final shake of the door, Sam heard her mom stomp away and slam her own bedroom door.

Sam sniffled and clutched her pillow even tighter. She had never gotten into a fight like this with her mom before, and her stomach was in knots. Clenching her teeth around her nail, Sam thought about running to her mom's room and apologizing until her mom forgave her and stroked her hair like she used to when she was little. But she didn't want to give her mother the satisfaction of seeing her buckle. She also knew that if she gave up now, nothing was going to change. Though, it didn't seem like anything was going to change anyway.

With a huff, Sam buried her head under the pillow and sniffed. She would do anything to have the notebook right now because all she would wish for is for her mother to disappear forever.

CHAPTER ELEVEN:
KYLIE
GROWING UP MEANS NOT
STABBING YOURSELF IN THE EYE

Why does being a girl involve so many tools?

Kylie was staring down at her older sister's makeup bag and blinking in confusion. She pulled out some sort of metal contraption that looked like a torture device and opened and closed it. Even though her sister called it an eyelash curler and had told her that it would help make her eyelashes look better, the idea of putting this thing near her eye made Kylie shudder, and she dropped it back into the bag. Who even decided that nice eyelashes even needed to be a thing? Who made these weird beauty rules?

She dug further into the bag and pulled out lip gloss and mascara, which were two tools that at least she was comfortable with. With her loot in hand, she rushed back to her room and quietly shut the door behind her. She didn't know how her sister would feel about her borrowing her makeup, but she didn't have the time or courage to ask her right now. Today they were going to be assigned their science projects, and if Kylie was going to get James to fall in love with her, then desperate actions had to be taken.

Kneeling in front of her mirror, Kylie uncapped the lipstick. At the bottom of the tube, it said that it was called 'Catch 'em Coral', and when she twisted the tube, she saw that the lipstick was a bright pinkish, orange color.

Carefully, she applied it to her lips. After making sure she hadn't smeared any on her face, she turned left and right, examining herself. She didn't know if this shade was 'her color' or what that even meant, but she could have sworn that her face looked a little brighter than usual, and it certainly drew attention to her lips, which she supposed was the main purpose of lipstick.

Next, she unscrewed the mascara and opened her eyes and mouth real wide so she looked like a fish. Kylie felt ridiculous, but this was how her sister looked when she applied her makeup, so it had to be right, right? Slowly, she applied the black goop to her left eye. Then as she was staring at her right eye, her mom screamed up to her from downstairs, "Kylie! Hurry up, or you're going to be late for school!"

Startled, Kylie jabbed the mascara wand into her eye. With a yelp, she tried to brush away the tears that had immediately welled up in her eyes. "Be right there!" she shrieked as she tried to brush away the black tears that started running down her cheek.

The black goop had smeared under Kylie's eye, making her look like a deranged raccoon, and the more she tried to clean it off, the messier it looked.

"Kylie! Down the stairs now!!!!" Kylie's mom screamed.

Frustrated, Kylie threw the mascara down on her desk, grabbed her backpack, and ran down the stairs.

"What was taking you so... Are you wearing makeup?"

Kylie tried to ignore the giggle in her mother's voice as she hurried out the door and sprinted to the bus stop.

The bus just pulled up as Kylie arrived, so she didn't have to talk to the rest of her neighbors as she threw herself onto the first available seat. Once she was sure she was securely seated, Kylie pulled out the tiny mirror from her backpack and inspected the damage.

It wasn't that bad, she decided. Sure, there was some leftover mascara still under her eye, but maybe James will think she was going for an edgy rocker look and think she was cool.

In fact, Kylie could have sworn that her eyes looked bigger and brighter, especially since she didn't have her stupid glasses hiding them, and her lips looked really bright and sparkly. Kylie couldn't look away from them, and she hoped that James would have the same reaction.

After a deep breath, Kylie forced herself to strut off the bus with her head held high to homeroom. Calmly she sat down and pulled the mirror back out of her bag to recheck that everything was in place. She couldn't wait for her friends to see it.

"Kyyyyylllimeeeee," Devin Mardson cooed, flipping her perfect long dark hair.

Kylie knew that Devin was one of the 'popular' girls, and by popular, it meant that Devin was naturally pretty and athletic, but terrifyingly mean. She was too cruel to win prom queen, and in twenty years, she probably would still be living in her hometown with a job she hated, clinging on to her high school days, but right now, she was not someone that Kylie wanted to talk to.

"Are you wearing makeuuupppppp?" Devin asked in the same tone one would use to try and lure out a wild animal while twirling her hair around her finger. Normally, Devin completely ignored Kylie, so warning alarms blared in Kylie's head as she started to scan the room for an escape route. "Your makeup is soooooo cute. You look adorable," Devin went on, smirking over her shoulder at her friends, who giggled behind their hands.

Kylie self-consciously touched her cheek, "You think so?"

"Absolutely. I mean, I think you are so brave for

wearing a lip color like that. I would never."

The girls behind Devin burst out laughing, and Kylie knew Devin was absolutely not being complimentary.

"I've always wanted to look like a drowned clown," Devin's friend called out, and the girls burst out into laughter again.

Fighting back her tears, Kylie raised her hand, grabbed her bag, and excused herself to the bathroom. Red-faced from tears and embarrassment, Kylie washed and rubbed away her makeup, all the while cursing herself for being so stupid as to think that she even looked good in the first place.

Gripping the edge of the sink, with her dark under eyes and red, raw lips, Kylie looked like she had been in a fight. There was no way she could go back to class and face Devin, and if James saw her like this... Well, he'd probably run away screaming.

Kylie heard the bathroom door open, and she ran into the stall, clutching her backpack, and tucked her feet up under her.

"Guys, stop. Seriously. I thought that it was cute that she was trying so hard."

Kylie recognized Devin's hideous voice coming from the stall next to her and cringed. Could this day be any worse?

"You're just saying that because you're dating James now, and you know she doesn't stand a chance," called one of Devin's friends.

Kylie's stomach dropped like she had just fallen off a high drop. There was no way that James would date someone like Devin. They had to be joking around. Right?!

"Seriously, she's always staring at him like a stalker. Once she finds out about you guys, you're going to have to make sure her weird friends and her don't put a spell on you or something."

"Uh, based on this morning, I don't think I have anything to worry about," Devin replied, and her minions giggled in response.

Kylie held her breath until she heard the door close. Then the dam broke and Kylie cried and cried.

What was she thinking? She was an ugly, boring freak. Of course, James didn't like her. He had probably been laughing at her with Devin behind her back for years.

Kylie wept, not caring that snot was starting to drip down her nose onto her shirt. She curled her hands into fists to keep them from shaking, and she ended up clenching so tightly that she could feel her nails making indents into her palm. Her face was so hot that she felt like her head was going to pop right off.

There was no way she could ever face James again. It was just too awful. Kylie wondered if she should pretend to be sick and have one of her parents pick her up, then just never come to school again. Or maybe she should just walk right out the school doors, into the woods across the street, and live the rest of her life as some sort of wood witch that people only spoke of in whispers around Halloween.

But as her breathing slowed, the waves of despair and nausea were replaced by an emotion Kylie had never felt before.

Pure, boiling, hot fury.

Obviously, she had been annoyed before. She had gotten frustrated with her siblings when they took her things without permission. She had been upset with her parents; she had even had moments of frustration when her friends talked over her. But she had never really been angry before. But, boy, was she ever angry now. It was the kind of anger that she had only ever read about. It was the kind of rage where all she could see was red, and there was a roaring in her ears.

Without thinking, she reached into her bag and pulled out the notebook and a pen. At this moment, she didn't care that she had already made a wish. She didn't care about the rules of the winsome foursome. She didn't care about consequences or doing the right thing. The only thing that Kylie cared about was hurting Devin and all of her stupid followers. With her pen poised carefully over a blank sheet of paper, Kylie wrote down the first thought that popped into her head.

I wish that all of Devin's hair would fall off.

Nothing happened at first, and Kylie wondered for a brief moment if the notebook wasn't going to work because she had already made a wish. But then, the notebook glowed brighter than it had ever done before, and the words faded away in an instant.

Kylie sat frozen, unsure of what she should do next. When suddenly, over the intercom, she heard the secretary's booming, bored voice.

"Kylie McHardy, please report to Mr. Beck's room immediately."

Kylie shot up and shoved the notebook into her bag. At this rate, she'd already missed homeroom, and God only knows how much of first period. She practically sprinted down the hall to Mr. Beck's class. Kylie had never been a particularly fast runner, but she was going so fast that her vision was actually starting to blur.

When she was outside of Mr. Beck's door, she took a moment to catch her breath before she had to face the humiliation of facing her classmates. But even as her breath slowed, she noticed that her eyesight was still as blurry as when she was running.

It was almost as if... Kylie gasped and fumbled in her bag until she found her old glasses. As she placed them on her nose, the world came into crystal clear focus.

"Oh no..." Kylie gasped just as a piercing scream came from the other side of Mr. Beck's door.

CHAPTER TWELVE:
JACKIE
EVEN WITH MAGIC, MIDDLE SCHOOL IS THE WORST

By second period, everyone was talking about Devin and her hair. Some people claimed that she went crazy and started pulling it out herself; others said that someone had put rat poison in her shampoo, and that's what made her hair fall out. No one knew for sure what caused it, but what was certain was that in Mr. Beck's science class, Devin was swishing her hair around like she always did, and all of a sudden, a huge clump of hair went flying across the room and smacked Travis Berkenson across the face.

The whole class went silent and froze, except for Travis who started gagging like crazy. Devin apparently went wide-eyed, ran her fingers through her hair. Then a few strands slipped onto her desk. Then a couple more. Until chucks of her hair slipped off her head like a waterfall.

Brianna Demois, the class gossip, told everyone that Devin went into a robotic state, and just kept pulling and pulling on her hair until she was half bald, and then all of a sudden, she started screaming like a lunatic and crying.

"She was totally hysterical," Brianna said to anyone who was in earshot, "Mr. Beck tried to calm her down and send her to the nurse, but she wouldn't move. She just sat there with her little patches of hair screeching. Mr. Beck had to call the office to get someone to get her. It was terrible," Brianna added, her tone implying that she thought that it was anything but terrible.

While everyone else was snickering behind their hands, Jackie didn't find any humor in this situation. Because while everyone else was theorizing what had happened to the class queen bee, Jackie had a pretty good idea she knew *exactly* what had happened, and she was furious. Not annoyed, not angry, Furious. It didn't take a lot to make Jackie angry, she always had a reputation as being kind of a hothead, but she had never felt so betrayed in her life. The second she had a chance to get to her phone, she sent a frantic text to the other three girls.

> *Jackie-*
> *Plan to Meet in the Bathroom at 11. Kylie bring notebook!!!*

Jackie watched the clock like a hawk through period three. By period four, Jackie was practically vibrating out of her seat, she was so impatient. The second the clock turned eleven, Jackie threw her hand in the air, "I need to use the bathroom!"

Her teacher blinked in confusion, but then gave an awkward nod of consent. Jackie practically ran out of the classroom, ignoring a couple of her classmate's rude comments. She didn't care if people were going to laugh at her; Jackie had to get to the bottom of this situation immediately.

Sam was already leaning against the sink when Jackie burst through the door. Sam raised her eyebrows at her, "What's up? I'm missing Gifted for this."

"Did you hear about Devin?" Jackie replied breathlessly.

Sam laughed, "Hasn't everybody?"

"Yeah, it's unbelievable, isn't it? It's almost like *magic*." Jackie emphasized the last word and gave Sam a meaningful look.

Sam shook her head, "There's no way this was Kylie. She would never break the rules like that."

The bathroom door swung open, and Sam and Jackie froze until Kylie's dark hair came into view.

They both relaxed until they saw the nervous look on Kylie's face, which was barely disguised by her old glasses. "Teresa is on her way here," Kylie muttered, "It takes her a while on her crutches."

"We'll catch her up," Jackie sniped. She had never been angry at her friends before, but right now, she wanted to take Kylie by the shoulders and shake her. "Did you hear about Devin?" Jackie pressed.

Kylie looked down and fiddled with a strand of her hair, "Yeah, it's wild, isn't it?"

"Yeah, it sounds like it was almost like magic," Jackie replied, folding her hands across her chest. Sam looked at Kylie with an expression not of anger, but disappointment.

Kylie was quiet for a second, but even with her head bent down, she couldn't disguise the tears that started rolling down her cheeks. "I... I know I messed up. Please just let me explain," Kylie sniffed.

"Kylie!" Jackie exclaimed, "We had rules! You already made a wish! How could you do this?!"

"I know. I know," Kylie cried, "I was going to tell you guys after school. I just wanted a chance to put my explanation together."

The door opened, and all the girls turned to see a bewildered-looking Teresa taking in the scene before her. "What's going on?" she asked. But Jackie caught Teresa's careful tone and the way her eyes carefully assessed her and Kylie's facial expressions.

"You know why we're here," Sam said matter-of-factly.

Teresa nodded slightly, and Jackie continued on her

rant, "How could you have been so selfish, Kylie?! I know Devin sucks, but this is actual magic! I found it! I shared it with you guys because I thought I could trust you! But you go ahead and do your own thing without even bothering to ask us!"

Kylie was fully crying now. Jackie watched as Teresa rubbed her shoulders reassuringly. But Jackie didn't feel bad, her stomach was in knots, and her entire body was shaking with anger.

"Devin said some stuff to me this morning, and I... I... I was just so angry. I wasn't even thinking. I just wanted to hurt her. I'm sorry. I'm so so sorry."

"You're sorry!" Jackie screamed.

Teresa cringed as Jackie's voice echoed through the room, "Jackie, calm down. It's going to be okay. They're never going to figure out it was us."

"I'm not worried about getting in trouble!" Jackie yelled, "I care about the fact that we have been given something special, and you are throwing away everything! We don't even fully understand how this works yet! And it's not fair that you get two wishes while the rest of us have taken our turn! Does this mean we all get an extra wish? What if the notebook doesn't even work any more?"

"Jackie, calm down," Teresa insisted, but Jackie didn't want to hear it. She was so hurt she wanted to tear the entire bathroom down tile by tile.

"No! She knows what she did was wrong! I'm tired of you always taking her side. It's obvious that Kylie is the only one you actually want to be friends with."

"That's not true!" Teresa groaned, "I just think you're overreacting. Yes, Kylie made a mistake. But we can fix this. I'm just trying to calm everyone down so we can think about all of this rationally."

"She wasn't being rational when she broke our rules!" Jackie snarled. Jackie could not and would not listen to Teresa. She was too upset. She wanted to hurt anyone who had betrayed her. To be honest, she wanted to attack anyone who was even in her general area. "Ever since you made your wish, you've been so different, Teresa!" Jackie screeched, "You think you're so much better than the rest of us now."

Kylie was fully sobbing, and Teresa crossed her arms across her chest, "Jackie, I know you're upset, and you have a right to be, but you're being really nasty right now, and it's not fair," Teresa argued. Teresa turned to Sam, who was watching the whole scene with an unreadable expression on her face.

"Sam, what do you think? You haven't said anything so far," Teresa asked, half pleading with Sam for backup.

"Don't bother," Jackie cried, "She's no help. She's been weird all day."

"Where's the notebook?" Sam asked, sounding strangely calm.

Trembling, Kylie reached into her bag and handed the notebook to Sam. Jackie reached for it, but Sam pulled it away before Jackie could lay a finger on it.

"Sam! Give it to me! It's mine!" Jackie whined, "I wish that I had never shown you guys this notebook. I'm the one who found it. Now give it to me. This isn't fun anymore, and I never want to use this stupid book ever again!" Jackie stamped her foot. She was being a complete brat right now, but she was too far gone now to care.

Sam didn't react to Jackie's tantrum but instead pulled a pencil out of her pocket.

"Sam, what are you doing?" Teresa cried and reached for Sam, but she stumbled on her crutches and would have face-planted if Kylie had reached out and caught her.

Without responding, Sam opened the notebook and scribbled something down before any of the other girls could react.

"Sam, stop!" Teresa yelled. But the notebook turned golden, and the glow burst forth brighter than ever.

Once the light subsided, the three girls turned to Sam, who was staring at the notebook and panting like she had run a mile.

"Sam..." Kylie whispered, "What did you do?"

Sam's face was white when she looked up, and when she spoke, it was so quiet that Jackie wasn't sure she even heard her correctly at first.

"Guys... I think I just made my mom disappear." Sam then slammed the notebook shut and covered her mouth with her hand.

CHAPTER THIRTEEN: TERESA
THE BREAKING OF THE FOURSOME

The girls stood in the bathroom in horrified silence.

"You what?" Kylie whispered.

"Why would you do that?" Teresa asked, wide-eyed.

Jackie didn't say anything, but she stomped over to Sam and ripped the notebook out of her hands, "How are you going to explain this? Your dad is going to freak out! He's probably going to call the cops!"

Teresa could feel her breath hitch in panic. Could they go to jail for this? Oh, God. Her mom would kill her if she went to jail, and her chances of any sports scholarships would be right out the window.

"Let them come," Sam replied stubbornly. But Teresa could hear the note of concern in her voice, "I'm tired of living under her control. It's always about what she wants, she never cared about me anyway; she just cared about sounding good to her friends. Well now, I'm going to start doing what I want."

"We can fix this," Teresa squeaked, looking back and forth, "We can fix all of this." Her mind raced to think of a logical solution to this absolute mess of a day.

"How do you suppose we do that?" Jackie barked, clutching the notebook against her chest.

"Don't you see," Teresa explained, "We can clearly make more than one wish at a time, but it erases the last wish that you made. Sam just needs to wish for her mom to come back, and Kylie just... well, I don't know... I guess you can wish for Devin's hair to come back. It'll be like today never happened."

"What if I don't want to undo my wish," Sam sniffed, "This might be my only chance to actually be free and to be an artist."

"I'll do it," Kylie whimpered, and she reached towards Jackie, who turned away.

"Who said that I would ever let you traitors use *my* notebook ever again?"

"Jackie, come on. I totally get why you're mad, but this is serious. Just let Kylie and Sam make their wishes, and we'll make things better. We can even hide the notebook, take a little break for a while until we all get our heads on straight."

"Take a break? Oh, we'll take a break. I am never letting any of you ever touch this notebook ever again." There were tears in Jackie's eyes, but the rage in her voice made it clear to all of them that her emotion was anger, not sadness.

"I thought you were my friends. I thought this was something we could share as, like, a symbol of our friendship or whatever. But you guys have taken total advantage of it. Now you've ruined all of the fun, and you've taken all the magic out of it. So now you have to live with the choices that you've made!"

"Jackie... We're your friends," Teresa whispered as Sam leaned against the wall and bit her nail. They had heard Jackie rant and rave before, but she had never yelled at any of them like this.

"I'm so sorry," Kylie cried.

Behind them, the bathroom door opened just as Jackie screamed, "I don't want to hear it!"

The door slammed shut, but Jackie didn't seem to care about strangers hearing her tirade.

"You are never going to see this notebook again, and I am never going to speak to any of you ever again! Deal with it!"

With the book still in her arms, Jackie ran out of the bathroom, leaving the other three girls open-mouthed in shock.

Teresa looked at Kylie, who was sniffing pitifully next to her, and back to Sam, who was staring at her feet. Frustrated, Teresa groaned and placed her head in her hands. Then, after a deep breath, she looked up and addressed the two girls as calmly as she could.

"We know Jackie. She blows up, but after a while, it'll be like nothing ever happened. We just need to give her time to cool down."

"What if she doesn't calm down?" Kylie whispered, "Yeah, Jackie has a temper, but I've never seen her this mad."

"Well..." Teresa looked to Sam for help, but she seemed lost in her own world, "Then we'll think of something to make all of this better. We're going to get through this. We're the winsome foursome. We have to, right?"

When Kylie and Sam didn't respond, Teresa let out a deep sigh and hobbled out the door. On her way back to class, Teresa's stomach was in knots, and she felt like she was going to throw up. Desperate to do something, her mind was spinning a mile a minute as she tried to think of her next move.

But even with her new and improved magical brain, Teresa found herself drawing a blank, except for one indisputable fact.

Seventh grade sucked.

CHAPTER FOURTEEN:
SAM
BE CAREFUL WHAT YOU WISH FOR

The rest of the day was a horrible and surreal blur. For about three seconds after she made her wish, Sam was so proud of her rebellion. But as soon as the reality of what she had done hit her, she regretted everything more than she could possibly say.

She tried to smile at Jackie in English, but Jackie refused to even look at her. Lunch was even worse. Kylie, who was inconsolable in the bathroom, later that day had been sent to the office and then, for one reason or another, had been sent home. Jackie was nowhere to be found. So, Sam and Teresa just sat across from each other in awkward silence.

Sam thought giving her art teacher her forged permission slip would make her feel better, but when her teacher read over the paper with a raised eyebrow, Sam couldn't shake the feeling of shame that washed over her.

The ever-practical part of Sam's brain kept telling her that this couldn't last. They were best friends, and Jackie would have to talk to them again, but no matter how many times she tried to tell herself that, she couldn't shake the feeling of dread that enveloped her.

On the bus ride home, Sam sat frozen as the horror of what she had done began to truly sink in. When Sam got to her stop, her descent down the bus steps was like walking to the executioner's ax. Trembling, Sam unlocked the front door and inched her way inside.

"Hello..." Sam called nervously.

"Hey, honey!" Sam's dad called back in a jolly tone, "I'm in the kitchen!"

With a gulp, Sam started to walk toward her father's voice. As she moved through the house, Sam started to notice little differences. A table moved to the opposite end of the hall. Cobwebs draped in usually spotless corners, and family photos were replaced by images of Sam and her dad on vacations that Sam couldn't remember.

There were no pictures of Sam's mom. There was no sign of Sam's mom at all.

Peeking into the kitchen, Sam noticed that the familiar red and white decor was changed to a hideous puke green and yellow. Her father, now bearded and beer-bellied, was humming to himself as he whisked eggs in a bowl. If he had noticed that his wife was missing, he sure didn't seem upset about it.

"Hope you're hungry, honey! I was thinking of breakfast for dinner! I hope that's alright with you."

"Yeah... That sounds great." Sam felt like she was in a dream. She was clearly in her house, and her father was definitely right in front of her, but everything was a little bit off.

"Um, Dad. Where's Mom?"

Sam's dad froze and gave Sam an expression of confusion and hurt, "What are you talking about, honey? If you're trying to be funny, I got to be honest; I'm not finding the humor here."

"I'm sorry..." Sam continued trying to word her question carefully, "I got a little dizzy in school, and I've had trouble remembering things all day. Can you remind me about Mom?"

Sam's dad placed the bowl on the counter and placed his hand on Sam's forehead, "Dizzy, you said? When did this start? Have you been drinking enough water? Do you want me to make an appointment with the doctor?"

"No. No," Sam insisted, "I'm fine. It's just been a weird day. But seriously, I don't mean to upset you, but please tell me where Mom is."

"Well, I wish I knew, sweetheart. You know that." Her father answered with clear concern.

"What do you mean?" Sam pressed.

"Well honey, when you were a baby, you just appeared on my doorstep. I actually don't know who or where your mom is."

Startled, Sam took a step backward. On one hand, this was better than her dad being worried and upset, right? But, on the other hand, her dad loved her mom, and there was something terribly sad about him not even knowing that she existed.

"Oh..." Sam trailed off, unsure what to say next. This day had been all too much, and Sam needed time to think.

"Yeah, sorry, I've just been off all day. If you don't mind, I think I'm going to lie down for a little bit before dinner."

"Of course, sweetheart," Her dad replied with clear concern written across his face, "There's headache medicine in the bathroom cabinet if you need it."

Sam nodded and tried to force a smile, but her facial muscles felt frozen in place. Hurriedly, Sam scurried to her room and threw herself on her bed.

At first, her room seemed to be the one place in the house that had been untouched by her mother's disappearance, but upon closer inspection, Sam could see small changes that made her stomach squirm.

The pile of Mandarin homework that she kept neatly on her desk had been replaced by a heap of scribbled drawing paper. There was no sign of her cello, and the carpet looked like it hadn't been vacuumed in months.

"Ok," Sam whispered to herself, "This isn't so bad. It's not like anyone's in pain, and I don't have to figure out an alibi for the police. I mean... This could work. I mean, isn't this exactly what I wanted? This might be a blessing in disguise."

With a deep breath, she rolled over to her side and pulled out her phone. She was hoping for some sign of forgiveness from Jackie or a hint as to why Kylie had been sent home, but the only person who had contacted her was Teresa, asking her what they were going to do. There was nothing at all from Kylie or Jackie.

Sam shoved her phone under her pillow and groaned. She knew Teresa meant well, but she didn't have the energy right now to talk with her, let alone try and think of some sort of plan. She pulled her covers up to her chin and closed her eyes. She was about to drift off to sleep when her dad called her for dinner.

Bleary-eyed, Sam made her way to the dinner table, and not even the sight of piping hot pancakes could cheer Sam up. Because as she looked across the table, she saw the empty chair that was her mom's usual spot.

Her father sat next to her and began chatting about his day, but his words were nothing more than a buzzing in her ears as she cut up her pancakes into teeny-tiny pieces. But it didn't matter how tiny she made the pancake slices. The lump in her throat didn't allow her to swallow, and all she could taste was the aftermath of salt as tears started to well up in her eyes.

It was strange and unnerving that her mom wasn't at the table, and Sam's stomach turned when she realized that her mother would never be across from Sam ever again. She tried to swallow her pancake, but her throat felt tight, and she started to gag and choke.

"Honey, are you alright?" her father asked in concern as Sam began smacking at her chest and gulping down water.

"Yeah," Sam eventually rasped. Once she managed to catch her breath, Sam placed her fork down on the table. "I'm alright, Dad. I guess I just don't have much of an appetite tonight. Do you mind if I go take a nap?"

"Not at all," her dad replied, forking her remaining pancake onto his plate, "If you need anything, just call, okay?"

Sam forced a smile and practically sprinted to her room. After ensuring that her door was shut and secure, Sam burst into tears that she couldn't quite explain and sank against the wall.

She wanted her mom. She didn't even know why. This was exactly what she wanted. She should have been thrilled, but everything about this world seemed hollow and strange, and all she wanted now was a hug from her mom, and there was nothing she could do about it.

Sam wept until her eyes were sore, and snot ran down her nose. She cried until she fell asleep right against the wall. It wouldn't be until hours later that Sam would see how her phone had lit up again and again as her friends sent her one desperate text after another.

CHAPTER FIFTEEN:
KYLIE
SOMETIMES TEARS TURN INTO PUNCHES

This had been the worst day of Kylie's life, and she was absolutely exhausted. When Kylie returned to class after the fight with Jackie, Kylie just plunked herself down in her chair and closed her eyes. How could one day go so wrong? She had lost her friends, her crush, and the most amazing opportunity that she could ever dream of.

Devin wasn't in class. She had been taken away by the nurse, and her mom had come to pick her up and take her to the doctor. But even though she wasn't physically here, her presence was all around them, as she was the only thing anyone in her class was talking about. Especially her so-called friends, who seemed to be taking great delight in the whole situation.

Kylie hadn't been able to look at James in science class, even when Mr. Beck managed to get the class somewhat under control and assign their project partners.

Throughout class Kylie observed him, trying to understand what he was thinking. She couldn't help but notice that if Devin really was his girlfriend, he sure didn't seem upset about what had happened to her, though he had never really been particularly expressive.

Devin had to be lying, Kylie decided. Somehow, she had figured out Kylie's feelings for James, and she was just saying that to try to hurt her. Yeah, Devin was pretty, but there was no way that James could go for a girl like her. Right?

At the end of class, Kylie went up to James. She wasn't sure what she wanted or even what she was going to say, but she felt drawn to him as if an invisible rope was pulling her toward him. "J-J-James," Kylie muttered. He didn't hear her at first, or if he did, he ignored her. Kylie should have walked away right there and then, but she seemed to be possessed by some evil demon that was determined to have Kylie make the worst decisions possible today. "James," Kylie managed to blurt out a little louder.

He paused and looked at her over his shoulder, "Yeah?" he grunted. James had never been a man of many words.

"Is it... Is it true that you're dating Devin?" Kylie wanted to slap herself across the face. What was she thinking? Was there something in her sister's makeup that made people act like lunatics?

James made a noise that sounded like a combination of a cough and snort, and shrugged his shoulders. "I don't know. I guess," he murmured.

James's friends, who had crowded around him to hear the conversation, burst out in laughter.

"Why are you asking Kylie?" one sniggered.

"Aw, she's gonna cry again. Go on, James, give her a kiss and make her feel better," cried another.

"Nah, bro, she's like one of fifteen kids. She'll probably get pregnant if you touch her!"

James didn't say anything, but he smiled awkwardly at all of his friends. He started to walk away, and Kylie knew that she should have just let him go. But that red-hot fury from earlier in the day reared its ugly head, and once again, Kylie found herself not caring about the consequences. It was one thing to make fun of her, but it was a whole other thing when it came to her family. Enraged, she marched up to James and tapped him on the shoulder.

When he turned around, Kylie swung back with all of her might and punched him directly in the nose. It was a great shot; with all her siblings Kylie had to learn to fight, and she couldn't help but smirk as she heard a satisfying crunch. Then she stomped away, leaving James yelling and clutching his nose as all of his friends hooted and hollered.

During the next class, Kylie was not surprised when the vice principal showed up to her class and told her to come with him. At this point, Kylie really didn't care what was going to happen to her any more. As she followed the vice principal to his office, they passed by the nurse's office, and Kylie caught a glimpse of James sitting bent forward on a chair, holding a bloody tissue to his nose.

After her trip to the vice principal's office, Kylie ended up with two days of out-of-school suspension for fighting, and her mom was called to come pick her up. She didn't know what to expect on her drive home. She had never gotten in serious trouble before, and she wasn't sure how her mother was going to react. Usually, her parents were pretty laid-back, but Kylie knew her dad could have a temper. Her mom was more of a mystery.

Silence was apparently her mother's response to anger and disappointment. Her usually chatty and giggly mother didn't say a word the entire ride home. By the time they pulled into their driveway, Kylie was half praying her mom would just yell at her already. Somehow, that seemed better than sitting in this uncomfortable silence.

Her mom put the car into park and let out a deep sigh, "Kylie, what is going on? Hitting people? That's not you, at least not at school. Did that boy say something to you? Was he bullying you? You can tell me." She didn't look mad. She didn't even look disappointed. Kylie's mom just looked worried as she tucked a strand of hair behind Kylie's ear.

Kylie was sure there was no way she had enough tears to cry anymore today, but this display of motherly concern after everything that had happened that day was just too much. She sniffled and buried her face in her hands, "It's... just been a... really hard day," she sniffled into her palms. She was too ashamed to look at her mom at this point.

Her mom rubbed her back and unlocked the car doors, "It's okay, Ky. Just breathe. Why don't you go lay down for a little bit, and I'll bring dinner to you tonight. Does that sound like a plan?"

Unable to speak through her hiccups or tears, Kylie just nodded her head, and her mom stroked her hair.

"Alright, Ky, let's get you inside. If you need anything, or if you want to talk, please just let me know."

For the next couple of hours, Kylie just lay curled up in her bed, clutching her favorite teddy bear to her chest. Her mom must have told the rest of the family to leave her alone because, for once, she wasn't being bombarded by her younger siblings asking her if she wanted to play or her older siblings asking if she had seen one item or another.

There was no way Kylie was ever going to school again. She didn't care what her parents said. She would think of something. Maybe she could homeschool herself or go to some online school, or maybe she could just drop out of school. Kylie was really good at making friendship bracelets. Maybe she could start a small business selling bracelets for the rest of her life in her parent's basement.

Kylie pulled out her phone and swiped through TikTok, desperate to try to take her mind off the fact that she had ruined her entire life all in one day.

Just as she had started to numb her brain with weird cooking hacks, there was a light knock on the door.

"I'm not hungry!" Kylie called, keeping her eyes glued to the screen.

But she heard the door tentatively creak open. Expecting to see her mother, Kylie huffed and sat up, but was surprised to see her sister Clara.

"If you're here to yell at me about taking your makeup, I really don't need to hear it. It's on my desk.

Seriously Clara, I beg of you, just take it and go. I've had the worst day of my life, and I really don't need to be yelled at anymore."

But Clara gently closed the door and sat on the edge of Kylie's bed. "Mom told me a little bit about your day. Between you and me, I don't know why you did it, but I think it's kind of awesome that you punched that James kid. His older brother is in my grade, and the whole family is kind of a group of douchebags."

Kylie stared down at her red comforter, unsure of what to say.

"As for the makeup, I mean, I'm annoyed you stole it. If you had just asked, I totally would have let you borrow it, but it's fine. You can keep it. I have a ton. Maybe when you're not grounded any more, you can have your friends over and have like a makeup party or something," Clara offered kindly.

"That would be nice... If any of them were talking to me," Kylie replied, allowing her hair to fall in her face so that her sister couldn't see her expression.

"What do you mean?" Clara asked, but there was no response that Kylie could give her. First of all, she didn't want to talk about the fight in the first place, but more importantly, there was no way she could explain the situation without mentioning the notebook. Kylie lay on her side and clutched her teddy bear to her chest.

"Did you guys have a fight?" Clara asked gently.

Kylie nodded and hoped that Clara would get the hint and get out of her room. But instead, her sister laid down beside her and softly petted her hair like she used to do when Kylie was really little.

"Fights happen. Seriously, don't worry so much about it. My friends and I used to bicker all the time in middle school. Mainly over boys..."

Clara got quiet for a second, allowing Kylie the chance to speak up, but Kylie's mouth stayed clamped shut. "I'm sure by tomorrow, you'll all apologize, and you'll be thick as thieves again."

"I don't think it's going to be that easy," Kylie whispered.

Clara rubbed her back, "Well..." Clara drifted off in thought. Kylie knew her sister well enough to know that she was desperately trying to think of a solution. Her sister's teachers had always described her as a 'go-getter', and Kylie knew her sister wasn't going to leave her alone until she thought of some sort of 'solution' to her problem.

"What you need is something that will force you guys together so that you have to talk. Is there anything coming up at school? Like a dance or a sporting event?"

"We don't have dances in seventh grade," Kylie reminded her sister, "And Teresa would be thrilled to go to a sporting event, but Sam and Jackie would probably prefer to chew their own arms off." Kylie was feeling more and more exhausted by the second, and all she wanted was for her sister to go away so she could sleep forever.

"Well, then, we'll have to plan something ourselves. You know, Mom and Dad only stay mad for like four seconds before they're back to saging our rooms and having family meditation sessions. When you know the timing is good, ask Mom to have a sleepover."

"They won't come," Kylie whined, "Seriously, Clara, I've had a horrible day and all I want is to be alone right now."

"No to a sleepover? Man, this really was a serious fight. Well then, if you're worried that they won't come, we need to create a situation where they have no choice but to come. Maybe we can convince Mom or Dad to have a parent dinner or something. That way, their parents will have to drag them here. Or maybe you could pretend that there's been some sort of family emergency, like a family member or something died, so they'll feel bad if they don't talk to you."

"Clara!" Kylie cried out in horror. She never knew that her sister could be so devious. "That's messed up! You're lying and messing with people's feelings! Also, knowing me, I'll end up jinxing things, and someone will actually end up dropping dead, and it will be all my fault."

"That's why you don't say that an actual person that you know died! You make someone up!" Clara said, looking pleased with herself at her own quick thinking.

"Clara. I'm begging you. Please get out of my room." Kylie groaned, rolled onto her stomach, and pulled the pillow over her head.

"But..." Clara began, but Kylie cut her off.

"I said GET OUT!" Kylie cried, kicking her feet.

"Fine," Clara sniffed, "I was just trying to help."

With a huff, Clara bounded off the bed and slammed the door behind her.

Kylie let out a deep groan and closed her eyes, wishing that she could just fall asleep for a few years. She didn't want to die, but a short coma sounded like a vacation.

Eventually, she did end up falling into a deep, nightmare-filled sleep, including a dream where her teeth were starting to fall out in gym class, but just as her two front teeth fell into her palm, something woke her with a start.

Dazed and befuddled, she sat up in bed. After taking a few seconds to take in her surroundings, she saw that she had been asleep for three hours, but that didn't matter right now. She stared at her phone and saw that she had a bunch of messages waiting for her. She bit her lip, for something in her gut told her that something had gone terribly wrong, and she was almost afraid to see what it was.

It turned out that Kylie's instinct had been correct because once she could focus on the bold words that had popped up on her screen, her mind began to race.

Jackie-
> *The notebook is missing. Seriously. I've looked everywhere. If one of you took it you better fess up ASAP! Im not kidding!!!! This isnt funny.*

Kylie clamped her hand over her mouth. She didn't know what shocked her more. The fact that the magical notebook had disappeared, or that Jackie really thought so little of them now that she would honestly believe that they would steal from her.

There was no response from Sam, but there were at least five texts from Teresa defending their innocence and offering logical ideas as to where the notebook could be.

Kylie's mind raced. This was an emergency. If the notebook fell into the wrong hands, the results would be horrific! But where could the notebook be? Was it possible that Jackie had dropped it somewhere in the school, and now it was in the hands of some diabolical eighth grader who would use it as a way to see more boobs?

Jackie was an only child, so they didn't have to worry about a sibling grabbing it as Kylie did, but her dog was famous for tearing anything and everything it could apart. What if Archie was tearing apart their precious notebook as they spoke?

But as Kylie chewed on a strand of her hair, she couldn't stop thinking about the point Jackie had made back when they first made the rules for the notebook. They still didn't know much about how the magic of the notebook worked or if it had a mind of its own. What if they had offended the notebook, and now it had chosen to disappear as suddenly as it had appeared?

She sank back into her bed. Maybe this is what they deserved. Maybe they weren't responsible enough for such a gift. She started texting out this very thought, and she was going to tell the other girls that they should just let it go, but before she could press send, something inside of her made her pause. Maybe there was something to what her sister had said, not the faking a horrible emergency part, but the forced getting-together part. An idea started to form in Kylie's mind, and as she started to type furiously, she wondered if this disaster could end up being a blessing in disguise.

She pressed send and went back to chewing on her hair, waiting with bated breath for one of her friends to respond. After what felt like an hour, her phone binged, and with a racing heart, Kylie grabbed her phone faster than she ever had before.

After a few moments of texting back and forth, the ending that they had come to wasn't perfect, but a small smile still spread across Kylie's face because now there was hope. Not a lot, but a small sliver of hope that maybe, somehow, their friendship could be restored. Of course, that was unless Jackie decided to cut all of their heads off and mount them on her bedroom wall, which was a much more realistic possibility than one would think.

CHAPTER SIXTEEN:
JACKIE
SO ANGRY YOU'RE CALM

Jackie knew that she had a temper. Her mom used to regale her with the insane tantrums she used to throw as a toddler. It got to the point that all it took was one look at Jackie's face for her parents to know whether they should back off or not.

Though she got mad easily, Jackie never stayed mad for long, and she certainly had never gotten mad at her friends. But as she slammed the door to her bedroom, she was more furious than ever before, and there was no sign of her calming down anytime soon. With a growl, she tossed her bookbag onto her bed. She then threw herself into her desk chair and crossed her arms across her chest.

Ever since finding out that the notebook was magical, Jackie had been keeping a journal (in a separate notebook, of course) of what had happened with her and her friends and about her day-to-day life in seventh grade. It was Jackie's greatest wish to one day be a best-selling author, and she thought their adventures would make for the perfect story.

But now, as Jackie read through her work, she just felt disgusted with herself. How could she have allowed herself to be so naive? Her words seemed childish, and her face actually felt warm from embarrassment as she read over a section where she gushed over the characteristics of her friends. The words sounded like they were coming from a stranger, so in her rage, Jackie picked up her journal and tore out every single page. Then with relish, she took those pages and tore them into teeny tiny shreds. Once she was satisfied, she gathered up all the little pieces and threw them in the trash can.

But the peace she found from this little endeavor only lasted a minute. she needed more. She wanted to break things, destroy things, and make people feel as hurt as she did. Narrowing her eyes, she spun her chair so that she was facing her backpack. That notebook. The stupid, worthless notebook was the cause of all her unhappiness. Jackie had sworn to her friends that they would never be allowed to write in the notebook again, and Jackie was going to make sure they would never be tempted, not ever.

Jackie reached her arm into the backpack, but as much as she wriggled her arm around, she couldn't feel the tell-tale leather of the notebook. Confused, she grabbed her bag and turned it over so that all of its contents poured out onto her bed. She found her favorite pen, which she thought she had lost in the first week of school, and a smashed granola bar, but there was no sign of the notebook.

All of the anger in Jackie's body drained out of her and was quickly replaced by a rising panic. She shoved her whole head in the backpack. Nothing. She crawled on her stomach and peered under her bed. Nothing. She tore off her bedsheets and checked every inch of her desk. Nothing.

No. No. No. No. This couldn't be happening. Those words repeated over and over again in her head as she sprinted down the stairs. Retracing her steps as best as she could, she scanned the foyer floor for any sign of the notebook. Still nothing. She ran to the kitchen table, praying that maybe her parents had found the notebook in the yard or by the front door and it would be waiting patiently on the table for her.

But when she barreled into the kitchen, there was no notebook. All Jackie saw was her dad drinking a soda and scratching Archie's ears.

"Dad, have you seen a leather notebook anywhere?" Jackie asked breathlessly.

Her dad moved from playing with Archie's ears to scratching his own chin, "A leather notebook? No..."

As soon as she heard the word "no" come out of her father's mouth, she tuned out everything else he was saying as her mind raced to try and think of where on Earth the notebook could be. "Uh, ok. Thanks, Dad. If you see it, though, please let me know, okay," Jackie choked out before she made a run for the door.

Outside, she scoured every inch of grass, but there was no sign of it anywhere. It wasn't in her bag, it wasn't in her room, and it wasn't even outside. At this point, Jackie felt like she was going to throw up.

Where could it be? Did it fall out of her bag on the bus? Could she possibly have left it in her locker at school? What if the bus driver found it and thought it was trash and threw it away? What if someone snatched it out of her backpack, and she didn't even notice? Pacing back and forth in the front yard, Jackie tried to think of what her next move should be. Could she call the school and see if someone found the notebook on the bus? Would they let her come after hours to check her locker? Could she interrogate every student in the school to make sure those criminals hadn't stolen from her?

After running back into the house, Jackie pleaded for her dad to call the school, but he wasn't having any of it.

"Jackie, I'm sorry that you lost your notebook, but first of all, it's after hours, so there's probably no one at the school to begin with. But more importantly, I'm not going to call and make a fuss and bother people over a freaking notebook. Besides, you have about eighteen notebooks up in your room as we speak. What's so special about this one?"

"It's got my science notes in it, and we have a test

tomorrow!" Jackie lied, but it was to no avail.

"Well, that's a shame, Jackie, but this is a valuable lesson about being more careful with your possessions. I'm sure if you ask around tomorrow it will turn up, but for now, why don't you call one of your friends for the notes? Sam's in your class, isn't she? I'm sure she'll share her notes with you."

"But, Dad..." Jackie whined.

"End of discussion, Jackie. I don't want to talk about this anymore. Honestly, I don't know why you're being so dramatic over this. It's really not that big of a deal."

Jackie couldn't tell him that it was a huge deal. She couldn't tell him that she may have lost actual, tangible magic. She couldn't tell him that she couldn't call her friends because they weren't speaking right now. She couldn't tell him that her whole life was falling apart and she was absolutely terrified. Nope, she couldn't tell him any of this. There were no words for how Jackie felt, so the only thing she could do was say nothing at all.

With a huff, Jackie spun on her heel and stomped up the steps to her room. After checking her backpack and her room one last time and coming up empty, she was at a loss for what to do.

The common-sense part of her brain was telling her that her dad was right and she would probably find it tomorrow. But that little voice was quickly overshadowed by images of the notebook being torn apart in a paper shredder. She couldn't wait for tomorrow. She just couldn't.

She paced the room to and fro, trying to plan some way she could break into the school in the middle of the night, but everything she thought of was ridiculous, even for her overly active imagination.

Jackie held up her phone and sighed. Desperate times called for desperate measures. So, swallowing her pride, sent out a text SOS to her friends. Relief washed over her when Teresa texted back immediately.

Together they went down the list of where the

notebook could be, and even though Teresa agreed with Jackie's dad and said that the notebook was probably at the school, Jackie still didn't feel any calmer. Teresa was just in the middle of going over the holes in Jackie's plot to wire down through the school roof *Mission Impossible* style when a text from Kylie flashed across the phone.

Out of all of her friends, Kylie was the one that Jackie had been the angriest at, but now reading Kylie's response, she couldn't help but smile in excited surprise.

> *Kylie-*
> *I've been in the school After Hours. Can promise that there are no laser beams. However, breaking in is not that crazy of an idea. Clara has key into school. Will explain later. I can sneak out around 9 and take a look around. Though we could cover more ground if were all there...*

Teresa was listing all the ways they could get in trouble if they went through with this plan.

Jackie didn't want to look weak by forgiving her friends right away, but she was so desperate to find the notebook she was willing to put her feelings aside for the moment.

Rapidly, Kylie and Jackie texted back and forth, and a plan started to come to fruition. Even Teresa eventually gave up on trying to talk the two of them out of it and ended up joining in the conversation.

In the end, the three of them came up with an idea that was so simple yet so crazy it just might work. All the rage from earlier in the day had drained out of Jackie and had now been replaced by pure determination. They were going to find the notebook, no matter what. After sending a final text, Jackie sat back down at her desk chair and began impatiently waiting for the start of their next great mission.

> *Jackie-*

??? ***I have questions about your sources
kylie. but... I'll see you all at 9. It's on.***

CHAPTER SEVENTEEN:
TERESA
NIGHT SCHOOL

This was crazy. No, it wasn't just crazy. It was stupid, moronic, and a complete recipe for disaster.

The first issue was sneaking out of her house in the first place. Even with two working legs, the task would have been difficult. First of all, Teresa's bedroom was on the second floor, and there was absolutely no way she could climb down. On top of that, Teresa's mom was a notoriously light sleeper and would definitely wake up if she heard the door open.

But with a busted leg on top of it, it seemed like there was no way that Teresa wasn't going to get caught. The only bright side was that if she did get caught, she was already stuck at the house without sports, so there really wasn't anything her mom could do to punish her.

However, it seemed that the gods were on Teresa's side. Earlier that night, her mom went to her monthly 'book club meeting', which was really an excuse for a bunch of the neighborhood moms to get together and drink wine. When her mom got home, she was particularly happy and sleepy, and she fell asleep face down on the bed right away.

After listening to the door and hearing her mom snoring away like a bear, Teresa decided that the coast was as clear as it would ever be, and hobbled her way down the steps.

Holding her breath, Teresa hustled her crutches across the carpet as quickly and quietly as she could. Then, after making sure that her house key was secure in her pocket, she opened the front door just enough for her to squeeze through, and she slowly clicked the door shut, grateful that her mom kept her door well-oiled, so there was no squeaking to worry about.

But getting out of the house was only the start of her problems. Now that she was outside, she had to figure out how she was going to get to the school.

Usually, this wouldn't be an issue. Teresa only lived about a twenty-minute walk away from the school. But that was when she had two working legs. On crutches, she would be lucky to make it to the school before the sun rose. Then she heard the sound of her knight in shining armor squeaking their bike horn down the road.

Barreling towards her was Kylie on her bike with a small red wagon weaving and bobbing behind her.

"Are you serious?" Teresa asked, blinking with confusion.

"Well, since I can't drive, this was the best I could come up with," Kylie explained, shrugging her shoulders, "My older siblings cart the little one around all the time this way. It'll be perfectly fine."

Teresa wanted nothing less than to get into that teeny wagon, but what other choice did she have right now? Swallowing her pride, she eased herself onto it and clutched her crutches tight to her chest. "If I break my other leg, I'm holding you and Jackie responsible, okay," she grumbled, desperately trying to find some sort of comfortable position.

With a grunt from Kylie, they were off, and by off, that meant they began to cruise down the road at a snail's pace. Normally, Kylie was the fastest of the foursome on her bike, but with Teresa's added weight and crutches behind her, Kylie's petite frame was struggling to make the bike wheel along. But with a crazed determination, they chugged on until they hit a hill, and Teresa's life flashed before her eyes as they careened downwards.

With a high-pitched shriek, Kylie braked as Teresa clung to the side of the cart and closed her eyes, praying that she wouldn't be flung off into the sky. By some unknown grace, they both made it to the bottom of the hill with all of their limbs intact.

After taking a moment to catch their breath, Teresa and Kylie saw that the school was now in sight, so with renewed energy, Kylie forced the bike forward while Teresa cheered her on. Eventually, they hauled their way into the school parking lot and saw Jackie's lanky frame outlined by moonlight. They tucked the bike and wagon behind the school dumpster so it was hidden from view, and they hustled as fast as Teresa's crutches would allow her over to Jackie.

"Where have you guys been?" Jackie hissed.

Even though her arms were crossed, Teresa could tell by the quiver in her voice that Jackie was scared.

Kylie pointed to Teresa, who shook the crutches in exasperation.

"I'm sorry I wasn't able to sprint here, your majesty," Teresa snarked, "In case you haven't noticed, I might be slightly slower than usual."

"Where's Sam?" Kylie asked, looking around.

"I haven't heard from her," Jackie replied, and the three of them stood in an awkward moment of silence as they wondered how Sam was dealing with her mom's disappearance and the consequences that choice may have brought.

But Jackie brought them all back to the business at hand.

"So, do you have the key?" Jackie demanded, sneaking a nervous look toward the school's side door.

Kylie reached into her pocket and pulled out a white piece of plastic the size of an index card.

"How on Earth did you get that?" Jackie gasped in

awe.

"There are some benefits to having a sister who is the most beloved student of all time. She got a key when she became class president, so she could come in and set up pep rallies, dances, and stuff for the high and middle schools."

"Does she know that you have that?" Teresa asked with narrowed eyes.

"I didn't exactly have time to explain the whole situation..." Kylie said awkwardly, "But I'm sure she would have been fully supportive."

Jackie and Teresa stared at Kylie with raised eyebrows.

"Well, if everything goes according to plan, she won't even know it was missing, and what she doesn't know won't hurt her."

"When did you become such a rebel?" Teresa said with a note of approval in her voice.

"Desperate times call for desperate measures," Kylie replied with a determined twinkle in her eye.

"Before we go barging in there, I did think of some things on my way here," Teresa added nervously, "What about alarms or cameras? I mean, it's great that we have the key to get in, but won't they have other forms of security? What if they check the cameras in the morning and see that we were in there? We can get expelled."

"Crap, you're right. I wish you'd brought this up earlier. Now we wasted our time," Jackie whined, biting her nail.

"There are no alarms," Kylie added confidently, "I've gone with Clara to help her set up like a thousand functions, and she's never had to deal with any sort of alarm."

"Okay, but what about cameras?" Teresa insisted.

Jackie threw her arms in the air in frustration, but Kylie placed her hands firmly on her hips.

"Well, we're here now,' Kylie declared, "And maybe they check the cameras every day, or maybe they don't bother looking at what happened during the night. We might get expelled, or we could totally get away with it. But we have to ask ourselves what we are willing to risk for the notebook. I mean, I don't know about you, but I'm willing to sacrifice an awful lot for actual magic. Especially magic that can restore our friendship."

Jackie placed her hands on her hips and nodded, "Let's do it."

Teresa shuffled her crutches around a bit before giving Kylie a thumbs-up.

With a final deep breath, the three girls quietly marched through the school doors. Teresa and Jackie braced themselves and held their breath as Kylie swiped the card against the black box to the right of the door.

When she saw the red light at the top of the box flicker green, Teresa bit down on her lip to keep herself from squealing out loud.

Kylie carefully opened the door, and the three of them stepped cautiously into the darkness.

There were no windows in the school hallway, so there weren't even rays of moonlight to help guide the girls down the pitch-black path.

"This is so freaking creepy," Teresa hissed, wishing she didn't have her stupid crutches clinking down the silent hallway.

"I can't see a thing," Kylie squeaked, and Jackie flicked on her phone's flashlight.

The school, normally filled to the brim with babbling students, was as quiet as the grave, and though it was freaky, Teresa felt a strange sense of freedom in having complete free range.

"Where should we look first?" Kylie whispered, wrapping her arm around Jackie for support.

"I hate to be the one who says this, but I think we should split up," Jackie muttered apologetically.

"I was afraid you were going to say that," Teresa grumbled, "And I'm not going alone. There's no way I can move on my crutches and hold my phone up at the same time."

The light from Jackie's phone gave her face an eerie mask-like appearance as she furrowed her brow in thought.

"You're right. The last thing we need is you falling down in the dark right now," Jackie declared, "This was my mess up, so I'll go alone. You and Kylie go together."

"I really think it would be better if we all stuck together," Kylie argued, but Jackie wasn't having it.

"We don't want to be here all night searching the school. If we split up, we'll be able to cover more territory way faster, and since I'm the one who lost the notebook, I should be the one to go solo."

"But where should we even start?" Kylie asked, "It could be anywhere."

"I'll start at my locker and then retrace the path I take for my afternoon classes. You two should start with the lost and found and then move on to the cafeteria. Make sure to stop and check every trash can you see in case some idiot tried to toss it."

"How are you going to get into the classroom? Aren't they locked? Also, what if they took out the trash already?" Teresa remarked, feeling nauseous at the idea of having to rummage through the dumpsters at the back of the school.

"They don't take the trash out until early in the morning. I saw the janitors doing it when I was at choir practice, and as for the doors..." Jackie pulled out a bobby pin, a paper clip, and her dad's credit card from her pocket, "Two years ago at summer camp, my bunk mates taught me every way you can pick a lock. Trust me; I've got this."

From there, it was decided. The girls would split up, and if they found any sign of the notebook, they would text each other where they could meet up. They also had to text every hour to check in. If the notebook wasn't found by 12:30, they would meet at the entrance and continue the search during school. This way they should, hopefully, have plenty of time to make it back to their houses and sneak into their rooms before anyone would be the wiser.

"I wish Sam were here," Kylie whispered right before they were about to separate.

After a beat, Jackie and Teresa replied, "Me too," in unison.

As mad as they may get at each other sometimes, they knew in their hearts that they not only needed each other in this tough, weird world, but they wanted to be with each other. They were the winsome foursome for life, and nothing was going to change that.

Hands slapped, and fingers locked in their familiar special handshake. With their friendship status now resealed it was time to bring the magic back into their lives, even if that meant creeping around the dark, spooky, probably haunted school.

* * *

Teresa and Kylie watched Jackie disappear into the darkness. When they couldn't hear the sound of her footsteps any longer, they looked at each other and shrugged.

"So... the lost and found? I mean that seems to be a good place to look if you're trying to find something... you know... lost," Kylie suggested, and Teresa grunted in agreement.

The lost and found was located in a small closet next to the nurse's office and almost at the opposite end of the school. The two of them walked in silence, their ears straining to pick up even the slightest of noises. The rumble of the air conditioner made them jump out of their skins more than once.

It felt like it took hours to finally get to the nurse's office. It was slow going in the pitch-black hallway, between only the faint glow of Kylie's cell phone to help lead their way, and Teresa's crutches slowing them down even further.

But finally, they reached their destination, and Kylie pulled a bobby pin out of her hair. After a few seconds of fiddling around, Teresa heard the click of the door unlocking, and Kylie slowly creaked open the door.

Quickly and quietly, they shuffled through gloves,

hats, old coats, smelly sweatshirts, battered backpacks, and even a pair of old cleats. But there was no notebook.

On the top shelf, Teresa found a stack of papers, notebooks, and folders. Holding her breath, she flipped through page after page, discovering science notes, math binders, pages of doodles, and even an eighth grader's diary, but no sign of their notebook. There wasn't a hint that it had ever been there and not a sign of where it could be.

"Any luck?" Kylie whispered.

"Nope," Teresa sighed, exhaling the breath she had been holding as she looked through the closet.

Kylie checked her phone for any update from Jackie, but there was nothing from her yet.

"I guess the cafeteria's next," Kylie said, but even though she didn't say anything, Teresa could hear the doubt and sadness in Kylie's voice.

With a sliver of determination, they headed towards the cafeteria, which was one floor below them.

Though it was not far, Teresa was not looking forward to finagling her crutches down the stairs. With Kylie's help, she made her way downwards one step at a time. With each move, Teresa had to fight the mental image of herself tumbling down the stairs, breaking all her other limbs, and having to wait in pain at the bottom of the steps until someone found her.

However, maybe the magic of the notebook was somehow still with them because Teresa made it to the cafeteria without any stumbles or falls. The cafeteria was normally bursting with noise and blinding with its bright lights. It felt like a ghost town in the quiet dark, with only the faint smell of cheap pizza and hash browns lingering in the air.

Teresa trailed after Kylie as she shone her phone up and down the long tables. They checked every seat and every corner. They snuck behind the counter where the cafeteria ladies usually dwelled. Even though they discovered bags of frozen nuggets and crates of milk containers, there was no sign of the notebook.

"You know we could steal as much food as we want right now," Kylie whispered as she rummaged through a box of apples.

"Yeah, but do you really want to choose to eat any of this stuff?" Teresa asked, turning her nose up at a strange-looking container. She didn't even want to know what was moldering in there.

"Good point," Kylie responded, and they continued their search. Which, to their disgust, included picking through the large red trash cans at each end of the cafeteria.

They found banana peels and apple cores. They found empty chip bags and half-eaten sandwiches. They even found someone's retainer and a pair of blue glasses, but again, not the notebook. They were disgusted, defeated, and most likely very smelly. They were getting tired, and this little adventure which had seemed so important and exciting was now becoming frustrating and exhausting.

"Well, what do we do now?" Kylie grumbled, slumping down onto a cafeteria chair.

"You haven't heard anything from Jackie," Teresa wondered, hopeful that Jackie had made a discovery and they could sneak home and take a well-deserved shower.

"Nothing, which is weird. I'm going to text her to make sure she's doing okay," Kylie murmured, and she began typing in her phone

Teresa peered over her shoulder and saw that just as Kylie was about to press 'send', a new text message notification popped up on the screen.

But it wasn't from Jackie. It was from Sam.

Sam-
Just got to the school. I'm outside right now. But Principal M is here with a cop and they're about to go inside. You guys better grab the notebook and run, or just plain run.

Suddenly, Kylie and Teresa weren't so tired anymore. They both just turned to each other, and even in the darkness, the look of terror was clear on each other's faces. The notebook was no longer at the forefront of their minds. They were both clearly thinking the same thing, for in unison, they both cried out in horror,

"We need to find Jackie."

Chapter Eighteen:
Sam
Does Anyone Actually Like
to Run?

Sam's friends were going to be killed. They were over, finished, doomed. For all the honors and Gifted classes Sam had taken in her short life, she couldn't think of any way they could get out of this mess.

Three of the winsome foursome were going to get caught, and they would get expelled, maybe even arrested. It didn't matter that they were considered good students for the most part. Breaking into school after hours was definitely going to get them into serious trouble.

Pacing back and forth next to the school, Sam tried to form a plan. Hopefully, her friends had gotten her message, so at least they knew what was coming, but there were so many details that Sam didn't know. Could they get out another door? Had they been caught on camera? Were they currently in one of the vents and were now trapped? Their bodies would end up being eaten by the mice in the school, and the hallways will stink, but the hallways always stink, so everyone would just assume it was pre-teen B.O., and no one will ever notice. They'll be up there forever, and their parents will never get closure. They'll make a true crime documentary about the three missing girls, and since Sam was the only one in the foursome who didn't disappear, she'll end up looking like the main suspect, and then not only will she not go to college, but she'll end up in prison for a murder she didn't commit.

She blinked a few times and shook her head. Man, she really needed to get out more, and she really needed to stop paying attention to those crime podcasts her dad liked to play when driving. Her head was getting seriously weird.

Refocused, Sam scanned the outside of the school. She didn't have a key like Kylie, so she didn't have a way of breaking into the school. The only hope she had was that Principal McKiney had left the door unlocked when he entered.

Hiding her bike behind a bush, Sam shakily crept down to the door and pressed against it as lightly as she could. When the door didn't budge Sam was about to turn back, but with a gulp of courage, she pushed against the door with an actual little bit of force, and it opened a tiny bit.

Holding her breath, Sam tip-toed into the school, her mind racing a thousand miles per minute. Okay, she thought to herself, I'm in. Now, what on earth am I going to do next? She had no idea where her friends were right now, so she couldn't just run around the school trying to find them, especially with the principal and the cops lurking around. She would definitely get caught before she could do anything of use.

If getting to her friends was out of the question, then the only thing she could do was try and deal with the main problem at hand.

It didn't take long for her to find Principal McKiney and the officer. For people who were on the hunt for some criminals, they weren't exactly being quiet about it.

Sam stared at the back of Principal McKiney's bald head and tried to think of a way to distract them without getting caught. The solution she ended up coming up with was not an elegant one. It was not well thought out, and to be honest, it was really, really stupid. But it was all Sam had at the time. With a deep breath, Sam engaged in phase one of 'Operation Distraction'. This involved kicking over a nearby trash can and screaming as loud as she could.

"They're over there!" screeched Principal McKiney.

Sam then knew that phase two was now in effect. Phase two was running as fast as she could. The key, though, was she had to be loud enough that they kept on her trail, but she had to run fast enough that she wouldn't get caught. Now, this would have been easy for someone like Teresa, who was a sports star and did weird things like actually running for fun. But Sam was not one of those people. Sam was a book-reading, cello-playing, Mandarin-speaking artist who walked the mile during gym class and lied about period cramps last year to get out of Field Day, though she hadn't even gotten her period yet.

Sam hated sports. She hated feeling sweaty and out of breath, so how she ended up in a situation where the future of her and her friends depended on her athletic ability, she'd never know. A stitch started to form in her side and sweat immediately started to pour down her forehead and into her eyes, blinding her. But still she ran on, the flapping sound of the cop's heavy shoes behind her egging her on further.

She had no idea where she was going or what her end plan was going to be. All she knew was that she had to keep running, even though it felt like her chest was on fire.

The footsteps behind her were getting closer and closer, and as much as she tried to push herself forward, her body wasn't cooperating. She was going to have to stop for breath, and she was going to have to stop soon.

Hopefully, her friends had time to get out of the school at least, Sam prayed as she skidded to a halt. She had reached a dead end. In front of her was a brick wall and two doors on either side of her.

She could hear the footsteps fast approaching, so frantically, Sam tugged on the knob of the door to her right, but it was locked. With no other option, Sam grabbed the handle of the left door and made a wish as she pushed as hard as she could.

CHAPTER NINETEEN: KYLIE WELL, WHAT DO WE DO NOW?

Jackie. They had to find Jackie, and they had to get out of there right now. Kylie texted Jackie furiously, but there was no response.

"We need to get to Jackie's locker right now!" Teresa squeaked frantically.

"Right! Go! Go! GO!"

As fast as they could, Kylie jogged, and Teresa limped up the cafeteria stairs, their ears straining for any sign of Principal McKiney. But all they could hear was the soft thump of Teresa's crutches and both of their weary pants as they clambered up the steps. Then, with a sharp turn, they hurried towards Jackie's locker.

"What are we going to do if Jackie's not at her locker?!" Teresa hissed.

"We can't think about that right now!" Kylie screeched, her heart pounding out of her chest at the very thought of it.

Kylie whirled around the corner. Spotting the outline of a figure down the hall, Kylie froze in place, forcing Teresa to bump into her back. Teresa managed to balance herself with her crutches, but Kylie was not so lucky, and ended up flailing to the ground in a huff, her phone skidding across the hall out of reach.

"Principal McKiney?" Teresa whimpered.

Kylie closed her eyes even though it was practically pitch black in the hall. She was too scared to see the rage on Principal McKiney's face.

There was no response at the end of the hall. Kylie wondered if he was plotting whether to expel them or arrest them first.

Kylie could hear Teresa inching a bit closer to the light, "Principal McKiney, if that's you, we surrender."

Surrender may not have been the word Kylie would have chosen at that moment, but she figured that it was better to just give up peacefully at this moment than try and make a run for it.

But still, there was no response. Digging deep down within herself, Kylie found enough bravery to open her eyes. Slowly, she made her way to her feet, her hands in the air, in case the figure was a police officer. Kylie really wasn't in the mood to get shot today.

When the figure before them still didn't move, Kylie started to wonder if maybe it was some sort of statue that they had never seen before. So, carefully, Kylie and Teresa moved toward the mysterious person. When they were finally close enough to Kylie's phone that she could reach down and pick it up, their eyes focused enough to see, to their great relief, it was Jackie standing in front of them the entire time.

"Oh my God, Jackie. Thank God it's you," Teresa exhaled with relief.

"What are you doing," Kylie cried, "We've got to get out of here now!"

Kylie rushed to Jackie's side and pulled on her arm, but Jackie would not be moved. It was as if she had been frozen into stone.

"Jackie, Come on! Did you see Sam's text?

After all this time, Jackie was standing in front of her locker. Kylie could see papers sticking out of the edges of the locker and that the whole thing seemed to be bulging forward from the rest of the lockers.

"It's in there," Jackie whispered, "I just know it. But my locker is completely jammed. I've put in my combination, like, thirty times, and it won't budge."

"Then ask a teacher tomorrow to help," Kylie whispered frantically, "We have to go."

"You don't understand," Jackie hissed, "This is bizarre. My locker wasn't like this when I left school. These papers came out of nowhere. It started sticking out of nowhere. This isn't just me being messy. This is magic, and I have this feeling; it's hard to explain, but I feel like the notebook is testing us, and if we don't get the notebook now, it won't be here tomorrow. It'll be lost forever."

"Well, if we don't hurry up, it will be gone because we will never be allowed in this school again," Teresa hissed, looking over her shoulder.

Kylie clicked the latch of the locker and found that it was unlocked. It was just stuck. A strange warmth started to travel up her arm, and she suddenly understood what Jackie was talking about. The notebook was in there. It was practically calling to her.

Kylie yanked as hard as she could, but the door wouldn't move. She tugged, and she tugged, but the door remained shut. "Jackie, try and help me," Kylie begged, "Maybe if we have more weight, we can get it open."

Jackie wrapped her arms around Kylie's waist, and together, they pushed. At first, the locker door remained unmoved, but just as they were about to give up, Kylie saw the crack of the locker start to widen a tiny bit.

"It's working!" Kylie cried, "Teresa! We need more weight!"

"Um, I'd love to help, but I'm a little unbalanced here," Teresa responded.

"Please," Jackie grunted, so with a sigh, Teresa dropped her crutches to the ground.

Balancing herself as well as she could, Teresa placed

herself slightly in front of Kylie, figuring it would be better to fall forward rather than backward. She then began pushing Kylie's shoulders as Jackie pulled her from behind.

Kylie was right. The locker was starting to open. The crack started to become a full gap, and Kylie could have sworn she saw the notebook's tell-tale golden glow inside.

But the slapping of footsteps sprinting down the dark hall made them all freeze in place. They didn't even have time to react when Sam barreled towards them, sweating and panting as if she had run a marathon.

"Oh, my God, Sam!" Teresa cried, her arms starting to shake.

"What are you doing here?" Jackie asked.

"What am I doing here? I had to hide in a janitor's closet until Principal McKiney left. I wanted to make sure you guys had time to escape. I ended up having to stand in a bucket of dirty water," Sam cried, "Principal McKiney will be here any minute!"

"The notebooks inside the locker," Kylie explained, "But the locker is jammed. We need to get it out!"

"Just get it tomorrow!" Sam hissed, "We need to go. NOW!"

But the other three girls didn't move. Jackie looked at Sam with pleading eyes.

"Just one more try. We're so close. If we don't get it this time, we'll leave. I swear," Jackie begged, "I think we just need one more person, and we can pull this locker open. Please, Sam, grab my waist."

Sam huffed and stomped her feet impatiently. Then with an exasperated sigh, she rushed behind Jackie and wrapped her arms around her waist.

"On the count of three," Kylie ordered, "Push as hard as you can."

"One," Jackie began.

"We don't have time for three! Just push already!" Sam cried, and on cue, the four girls pushed and pulled with all of their might.

Teresa grunted with strain, and Kylie's fingers were on fire, but the locker started to open wider and wider until, suddenly, it flew open, sending the four girls toppling to the ground.

After a second of groaning in pain, Jackie bolted up and reached up, snatching the notebook out of her locker holding it aloft.

"I've got it," Jackie exclaimed, "I have no idea how it got in there, but I've got it."

"We'll figure it out later. We've got to go!" Sam urged.

Jackie slammed the locker shut as Kylie and Sam helped Teresa to her feet. There was no time to catch their breath because they heard, around the corner, the static of the radio and heavy footsteps pausing to respond to a message.

"Go," Teresa whimpered, "I'll just slow you guys down.

"Yeah, right," Jackie responded, "There's no way we're leaving one of the foursome behind."

Jackie grabbed Teresa's crutches while Kylie and Sam practically carried Teresa down the hall as fast as their little feet could carry them. But Principal McKiney was faster, and they could hear his footsteps getting closer.

"There's no way we're getting out of here," Sam whispered.

She was right. There was no way they could possibly outrun him. But Teresa seemed to have an idea or a death wish because she wrenched herself out of Kylie and Sam's arms and dove toward Jackie.

"The notebook!" Teresa said as she wrenched the notebook out of Jackie's hands.

"Have you gone mad!" Jackie cried, but Teresa was busy patting Jackie's pant leg down. Until, with a cry of delight, Teresa pulled a pen out of Jackie's pocket.

Sam caught on to Teresa's plan, and she dropped to her knees and flipped open the notebook.

"Whose turn is it to go?!" Jackie asked.

"Who cares!" The other three responded as Teresa frantically scribbled away in the notebook. The sound of Principal McKiney's footsteps was so close; he'd be on them in a matter of seconds.

"I wish Principal McKiney and the cop would leave the school right now!" Teresa scrawled. She wrote so fast that the sentence was practically illegible, but still, the notebook shined on.

The four of them held their breath as Principal McKiney's pace slowed and the static of the radio buzzed again.

"How on Earth could they have gotten outside? I just heard them... Fine, I'll be right there."

Only when they heard Principal McKiney turn heel and stride a good ways away did they bother to exhale.

"Now, can we go?" Sam begged. And without another word, the four of them carefully snuck their way out of the school.

After tumbling through the school doors, the four exhausted, exhilarated, and sore girls took a second to breathe in the cool fall air.

After a moment of silence, Kylie began to giggle for reasons that she didn't fully understand. She was soon joined by Teresa, then Sam, and finally Jackie, until the four of them were hysterical with laughter, and tears of joy streamed down their faces.

After catching their breath, the four of them hopped onto their bikes, or in Teresa's case, her wagon. They began their journeys home, tired, but excited to see what the next day would bring. Because there was no way they could end their night without a few more wishes.

CHAPTER TWENTY:
JACKIE
THE YEAR HAS ONLY JUST
BEGUN

The fact that they all managed to somehow make it home without getting caught by their parents was a miracle. But the fact that they didn't get in trouble that night was pure magic.

As soon as Jackie, Teresa, and Sam arrived at school the next day, Principal McKiney pulled them into his office. (Kylie got to miss out on this little exchange since she was still suspended.)

"Ladies, I am here to inform you that last night a silent alarm was set off, and after examining the cameras, the police and I were able to determine that a group of students had broken into the school."

He stared at them meaningfully, waiting for a response. The three girls sat silent, trying to look as innocent as possible.

"At first, it was thought to be the work of four girls. Four girls from this very seventh-grade class."

He paused, an uncomfortable silence filled the air, but still, the girls did not break.

"Upon investigation, the police believe that it was

actually the work of four boys from a rival school district. The culprits were never found, but I can promise you that the police are taking this very seriously, and are continuing their search."

Again, there was a pause, and Jackie wondered where he was going to go with all of this.

"I personally am not fully convinced that this was the case, but strangely, the video footage is showing us nothing but static. I may not have any proof of what happened last night, but I am telling you, girls, that if you know anything, anything at all, about what happened last night. I suggest you tell me right here and right now. Because if we find out that you lied, the punishment is going to be much, much, more severe."

Principal McKiney stared each of them in the eye, and time ticked by second by second. Still, the girls were quiet, blinking in fake confusion.

"Nothing?" Principal McKiney, "Nothing at all?"

When he received no response, Principal McKiney sent them all on their way, but not without a final warning that he would be "keeping an eye on them."

Despite the dark circles under their eyes, the girls had gotten away with their crime. It probably helped that before they had biked away, Jackie had made a wish that they wouldn't get in trouble for breaking into the school.

In fact, they had made a series of wishes that night. Thanks to Kylie's wish, Devin returned to school that day with a full head of hair. She told anyone who would listen that she had a reaction to her shampoo but was fine now; however, behind her back everyone said that she was wearing a wig.

Teresa found that she didn't like this new smartie pants persona that she had created. Now that her previous wish had been erased, she was happy to embrace her jumbled head and quickly healing ankle. "I'm going to figure this school thing out on my own terms," Teresa had explained, "But, at the end of the day, I still want to be me. Besides, I have to deal with you brains enough as it is. I don't need any more."

Sam wished for her mother to return, but she promised herself she was going to start sticking up for herself more. Starting with telling her mom about her new art classes and how she wasn't going to be quitting them, no matter how much her mom insisted.

Jackie didn't know what to wish for. She didn't even know if she wanted to make a wish ever again, but after school, the winsome foursome returned to the original park where they had made the rules of the notebook, to begin with.

"Well, we're back to normal," Sam sighed, "Or as normal as we ever will be."

"What do you want to do, Jackie?" Kylie asked softly, "In the end, you were the one who found the notebook. If you never want to use it again, I would understand."

Jackie clutched the notebook to her chest as if she were holding a childhood teddy bear. In such a short time, so much damage had come from this notebook, the wise decision would be to hide it away for good, yet, she felt that the four of them still needed this notebook.

Jackie knew in her heart she hadn't put the notebook in her locker. It had chosen to go there on its own. Jackie also knew her locker had not gotten jammed on its own. No, the notebook had made those choices. The notebook left when their friendship had ended, and only returned to them when they decided to work together fully.

"I think we're going to have to make some adjustments to the rules," Jackie replied thoughtfully, "I definitely think we're going to have to be way more careful about how we use it, but... The notebook is a part of us now. It's more than just magic, it's a symbol of our friendship. I think as long as the four of us plan to stick together, the notebook will stick with us too."

"Well, I don't plan on going anywhere," Teresa

laughed, leaning her head on Kylie's shoulder.

"Neither do I," Kylie laughed as she braided Sam's hair.

Sam closed her eyes and tilted her head back further, "So it looks like we're stuck with the notebook."

"Or the notebook is stuck with us," Jackie grinned, "Besides, seventh grade just started, so it might be a good idea to have a backup plan. You know, just in case."

The park may have been the same, but the girls, now different than they had been before, renewed the rules for the notebook, but more importantly they renewed their promise of friendship. Even though they knew plenty more was still to come, the winsome foursome was not going to be broken any time soon.

Other titles by BLKDOG Publishing for your consideration:

Britannia: The Wall
By Richard Denham & M. J. Trow

THE END OF ROMAN BRITAIN BEGINS.

The story opens in 367 AD. Four soldiers - Justinus, Paternus, Leocadius and Vitalis - are out hunting for food supplies at an outpost of Hadrian's Wall, when the Wall comes under attack.

The four find their fort destroyed, their comrades killed, and Paternus is unable to find his wife and son. As they run south to Eboracum, they realize that this is no ordinary border raid. Ranged against the Romans at the edge of the world are four different peoples, and they have banded together under a mysterious leader who wears a silver mask and uses the name Valentinus - man of Valentia, the turbulent area north of the Wall.

Faced with questions they are hard-pressed to answer, Leocadius blurts out a story that makes the men Heroes of the Wall. Their lives change not only when Valentinus begins his lethal sweep across Britannia but as soon as Leo's lie is out in the world, growing and changing as it goes.

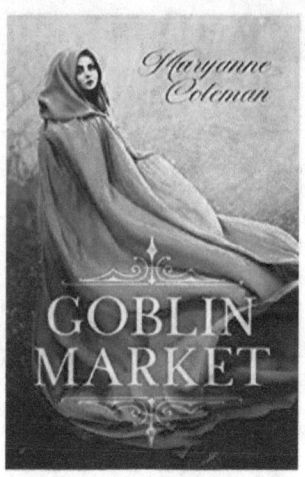

Goblin Market
By Maryanne Coleman

Have you ever wondered what happened to the faeries you used to believe in? They lived at the bottom of the garden and left rings in the grass and sparkling glamour in the air to remind you where they were. But that was then – now you might find them in places you might not think to look. They might be stacking shelves, delivering milk or weighing babies at the clinic. Open your eyes and keep your wits about you and you might see them.

But no one is looking any more and that is hard for a Faerie Queen to bear and Titania has had enough. When Titania stamps her foot, everyone in Faerieland jumps; publicity is what they need. Television, magazines. But that sort of thing is much more the remit of the bad boys of the Unseelie Court, the ones who weave a new kind of magic; the World Wide Web. Here is Puck re-learning how to fly; Leanne the agent who really is a vampire; Oberon's Boys playing cards behind the wainscoting; Black Annis, the bag-lady from Hainault, all gathered in a Restoration comedy that is strictly twenty-first century.

Fade
By Bethan White

There is nothing extraordinary about Chris Rowan. Each day he wakes to the same faces, has the same breakfast, the same commute, the same sort of homes he tries to rent out to unsuspecting tenants.

There is nothing extraordinary about Chris Rowan. That is apart from the black dog that haunts his nightmares and an unexpected encounter with a long forgotten demon from his past. A nudge that will send Chris on his own downward spiral, from which there may be no escape.

There is nothing extraordinary about Chris Rowan...

BLKDOG

www.blkdogpublishing.com